BE THE BRAND. Define It. Design It. Deliver It.

Published by BookSurge Publishing.

ISBN: 1-4196-3840-8

Printed and bound in the United States of America.
This book is printed on acid-free paper.

EDITORIAL DIRECTOR
Dr. Gregory Suss

COVER & BOOK DESIGNER
Sean Hayes Design, LLC

PHOTOGRAPHER
Papier Photographic Studios

ILLUSTRATOR
Flladi Kulla

DEDICATED TO

My mother, who created the brand;

My clients, who bought the brand;

My daughter, who perpetuates the brand.

BE THE BRAND™

Define It. Design It. Deliver It!™

Elevating the Status of YOU!™

TAMARA JACOBS

About the Author

Tamara Jacobs Communications, Inc. has been improving the presentation and communication skills of successful professionals across the country for over 20 years. Ms. Jacobs, President of Tamara Jacobs Communications, Inc., began her career in television during which time she was involved in writing, producing, reporting & anchoring at network affiliates on the West Coast, in the Midwest and Southeast. Also an accomplished actress, Ms. Jacobs has appeared in several Off-Broadway productions and national tours, and is a member of Actors Equity. She has combined her communications and professional theatre experience with recognized success in the arena of media and presentation training, appearing on such national programs as *ABC World News*, *The Fox News Network*, *The Gayle King Show*, *Extra*, *Entertainment Tonight*, and *Your World with Neil Cavuto*. She has also been featured in *Fortune & Your Company*, *Woman's Day*, *Woman's World* and *Victoria Magazine* as a preeminent expert in the field of business communication. Tamara has also recently served as a judge for the *Miss America Pageant*.

Tamara Jacobs Communications, Inc. offers seminars focused on presenter training, facilitation, executive presence, gender communication and business etiquette as well as media and Q & A preparation. Featured workshops include: Persuasive Presentations, Sell Don't Tell, D.R.I.V.E. - The Journey to Successful Facilitation™, The Feminine Force™, Projecting a Professional Image, Managing the Media and Business Etiquette.

Workshops are also available for event specific development, which in the past have included:

+ Speeches delivered at national meetings and conferences
+ Challenging media interviews on high-visibility programs
+ Preparing key opinion leaders for small and large group presentations
+ Perfecting sales presentations in the field
+ Conducting "Train the Trainers" programs
+ Implementing leadership development seminars
+ Internal presentations
+ Facilitation of small groups and workshops

Table of Contents

Introduction

If there's one concept you will take away from this book, it's that your physical presence and vocal effectiveness count for the vast majority of your effect on others, whether you're standing in front of a group in a formal presentation or having a brief one-on-one conversation. Authoritative studies have proven that how you look and how you sound (as opposed to what you say) add up to 93% of the equation. It's not about the size of the slide deck. It's not about clever animation or the number of PowerPoint bullets. It's not about copious handouts. It's about YOU!

With this in mind, do you feel you expend the appropriate amount of effort on your personal packaging™ and presentation impact?

An example to ponder: In the early 1900s, a product called "Cracker Jack" became synonymous with caramel corn. There were other such products on the market, including "Five Jacks," "Sammy Jack," "Yellow Kid" and "Goldenrod." How did Cracker Jack hold on to their market share when all of these competitors figured out how to make a similar tasting snack food in a wax-sealed, moisture-proof box?

What Cracker Jack did was to make their packaging memorable (as the precursor to McDonald's "Happy Meal") by giving away a hidden free toy in every box, along with the warm image of a sailor boy and his dog on the front as a wartime salute to our fighting boys "over there." As time went on, Cracker Jack and the *surprise inside* were inseparable. Millions of boxes were sold as kids all over America (you may have been one yourself) ripped open the wrapper to uncover the special free prize. The result was that Cracker Jack dominated the market and the copycats had to fold up their tents, all thanks to innovation and smart packaging!

When the 2004 baseball season opened, Yankee Stadium in New York City attempted to replace Cracker Jack with another caramel corn product, "Crunch 'N Munch," a hip newcomer with a snappy logo. Nobody wanted to sing "Buy me some peanuts and Crunch 'N Munch…" The fans' reaction was instantaneous and enormous! To avoid a riot, Yankee Stadium was forced to pull "Crunch 'N Munch" and return to "Cracker Jack" within a matter of days!

This same strategy is vital to how you go about packaging and presenting yourself to the world. You can be a highly eloquent, smart speaker, but because 93% is not what you say but how you sound and look, your presentation can still fail. Physical presence and voice are part of the total package - they go hand in hand. You can dress the part but fail orally, or vice versa. Both elements have to be working in tandem.

This book will offer time-tested methods on how to increase your awareness and improve your vocal, verbal and body skills. Simple adjustments will pay off in huge dividends. From everyday interactions to stand-up meetings, people will really pay attention to you, recall what you have to say and take the appropriate action. This applies to job interviews, performance reviews, office staff meetings, even talking a police officer out of giving you a traffic ticket; we're always onstage when we're interacting with others. And the most effective way to present is really not to present at all, but to construct an "organized conversation."

Regardless of your particular walk of life, success boils down to your ability to effectively communicate. Whether delivering the toast at a wedding, coaching a team, expressing your opinion at a local city council referendum, facing investors at a shareholders' meeting or pitching to a new client, presenting a "you" that is interesting, animated and personable is crucial to achieving the goal of the presentation.

In a recent issue of *Forbes*, C/Net Founder and current CEO of Grand Central Communications, Halsey Minor, stated, "The external role of a CEO is far more important today than ever before because the market, the press and the analysts have such a huge impact on the perception of a company and its brand." Later in the article, Ann Winblad, a founder of Hummer Winblad Venture Partners, added, "If the CEO doesn't appear to be a good communicator, we don't fund the company."

During the 2005 Conclave of Cardinals to select a pope following the death of John Paul II, many were quoted as saying that a major criterion for selecting the next pontiff would be his ability to effectively communicate to all nationalities and ages. While the deliberations of the Cardinals (in keeping with Canon Law) are strictly confidential, many, following the election of Pope

Benedict XVI, stated his mastery of many languages and his ability to reach out to the mighty and humble alike as key factors in his selection.

If you're shy when you communicate, this book can help you fix that. You will be shown how to look better and speak effectively. You will learn how to present yourself in an interesting manner and give people key factors to remember. Imagine what it will be like to make business presentations and speeches that will be what most are not - persuasive and memorable!

BE THE BRAND™ *Define It. Design It. Deliver It!*™ discusses the many secrets to achieving your life dreams, secrets that I've taught with great success in my many years as a professional communications consultant and media advisor. These techniques can help anyone fine-tune his or her public persona.

There have been many books written over the years about communication that tell you how to be an effective speaker. This book is very different - it discusses how to get beyond "yourself" in order to impact an audience. It's not about how to stand up onstage and check off a list of topics, but more importantly, how to impress, connect and engage the person or people with whom you're interacting. You can't imagine the sense of confidence, satisfaction and power you will derive from knowing that when you walk into a room, everyone will be interested and involved. They will remember what you have to say.

Before we continue, take a few moments to complete the following Individual Self-Inventory. This short personal evaluation will focus on 12 key areas of your communication style. Score yourself on a scale from 1-5 in each area - and be as honest as possible! After you've completed this book, I'd like you to perform this exercise again. I think you'll be amazed at the different scores you'll give yourself. It's not about perfection - it's about awareness! So, are you ready to get to work? Turn the page and let's get started!

Individual Self-Inventory
Test Yourself!

WEAK				STRONG

Personal Demeanor

1	2	3	4	5
Nervous				Calm
Edgy				Confident
Unfocused				Organized

Body Posture

1	2	3	4	5
Stiff or Slouchy				Erect
Awkward				Coordinated
Tense				At Ease

Hand & Body Gestures

1	2	3	4	5
Inappropriate				Appropriate
Distracting				Enhancing
Misleading				Clarifying

Eye Contact

1	2	3	4	5
Rarely Made				Continuous
Uncomfortable				Comfortable
Threatening				Welcoming

Authenticity

1	2	3	4	5
Closed				Open
Hidden Motives				Candid
Insincere				Sincere

Sensitivity

1	2	3	4	5
Doesn't Notice Reactions			Notices Reactions	
Doesn't Check Feelings			Asks About Feelings	
Doesn't Listen			Listens Intently	

Attending Behavior

1	2	3	4	5
Oblivious to Concerns			Responds to Concerns	
Offers No Feedback			Offers Observations	
Appears Glum			Is Upbeat and Positive	

Self Control

1	2	3	4	5
Overly Emotional			Appropriate Emotions	
Loses Temper			Remains Neutral	
Shows Displeasure			Stays Pleasant	

Flexibility

1	2	3	4	5

Doesn't Test | | | | Tests the Process
Alternatives Not Offered | | | | Offers Options
Forces Preset Direction | | | | Adjusts Constantly

Unobtrusiveness

1	2	3	4	5

Is the Focal Point | | | | Is Unobtrusive
Grandstands | | | | Avoids the Limelight
Talks Excessively | | | | Lets Others Talk

Focus

1	2	3	4	5

Gets Lost | | | | Pays Attention
Loses Key Ideas | | | | Manages Input
Seems Distracted | | | | Totally Engaged

Energy

1	2	3	4	5

Slows Down | | | | Maintains Pace
Seems Drained | | | | Is Energetic
Appears Wan | | | | Appears Robust

INTRODUCTION

1

The 30 Second Window of Opportunity™

"The knock at the door tells the character of the visitor."
T.K.V. Deiskachar

MISSION STATEMENT
During the first 30 seconds, your audience decides
whether or not they're going to listen to you.

I open every presentation with a mission statement that outlines the desired outcome. So, in these pages as in my work every day, I will begin each chapter with a mission statement. For this chapter, the purpose is to make you realize the *crucial importance of the first 30 seconds*, be it during a meeting, a conversation, a presentation, an appearance, - any communication effort! During the first 30 seconds, your audience decides whether or not they're going to listen to you. And, the clock begins ticking not when you begin to speak, but rather when you come into view.

The first 6 seconds is when an audience will assess you visually. In a nutshell, they 'check you out' from top to bottom. Whether you realize it or not, you do exactly that when someone gets in front of you to speak. You examine how they're dressed, if they look friendly, if they are happy to be there, if they appear to be confident. This initial impression is extremely important.

To that end, your hair and clothing need to be arranged before you get up to speak. I can't tell you how many times I've seen speakers introduced only to find them smoothing their hair, straightening their jackets, pulling up their trousers and other sorts of grooming moves as they make their way to the front of the room. This initial impact leaves the audience to wonder what else the speaker forgot to do before he or she left the house. Not a good way to start! Your **personal packaging**™ is of the utmost importance. Studies have proven that how you look amounts to 55% of your impact on an audience, large or small! While I devote a good deal of the next chapter to attire, it is not too early to point out that appropriate clothing and grooming go a long way to ensure acceptance by an audience during the crucial first 6 seconds. Shopping for your professional wardrobe should not be considered a frivolous exercise - it's business and needs to be taken very seriously. Your physical presentation speaks volumes about you and will enhance (or diminish) your credibility.

Smile!

Enthusiasm is infectious - if you don't have it, your audience can't catch it!™ Before you say a single word, take a moment to *smile* at the audience. In that first 6 seconds, the biggest single factor in making an impression is your smile. Since people usually mirror what they see, it is very difficult for somebody to look unpleasantly back at you if you are smiling at him or her. The smile relaxes your face (and you!), adds warmth and makes people feel comfortable with you (and without comfort, there's no credibility!).

Just think of how many times you've sat in a meeting or presentation and the speaker appears before you with an expression of complete lack of interest, or boredom, or oppressive gravity or, even more disastrous, extreme discomfort.

How does that make you feel? Don't you immediately look at your watch and start counting the seconds until the presentation is mercifully over? Think of what your face is capable of showing to the world. You can appear to be happy, but also angry, hostile, worried, bored, dispassionate, eager, enthusiastic, supportive, curious or calm. I'm sure you would agree with me that happy, enthusiastic and calm are the emotions your face should be portraying in most work situations.

One well-known study shows that 85% of success in sales isn't due to knowledge, but good old American positive vibes! "Charisma," notes corporate speaker Ralph Archbold, "is the transference of enthusiasm." Translation: **care** - and give the people with whom you come in contact a reason to care.

When I conduct seminars, I always make a point to walk onstage, say "Good morning," and project a big, bright smile. I'm happy to be there, speaking to my audience. And even if I weren't really happy, I better look like I am, or else I've lost everyone in the room immediately! By the way, remember when your mom used to say, "Smile, you'll feel better!" (at least mine did)? Well, she may just have been right. Apparently, there are approximately 80 muscles in the face capable of 7,000 different expressions (can you imagine being assigned to counting and cataloguing them?). At any rate, when you smile, it does release endorphins. Whether you've engaged all your facial muscle mass or not, you're still exercising a lot of them and experiencing a "lift" in the process. Feeling good and looking good go hand-in-hand, and I encourage you to telegraph them both!

Regardless of the subject matter, you want the audience to like you, and they will mirror your expression. Watch any local or national newscast, and you will see the anchor always greeting the television audience with a smile before he or she assumes a more serious demeanor, even if the lead story is extremely grave. We encounter very stern, angry, nervous or blank expressions at every turn, and we are put off by them. The best way to ensure that others will not interact with you is by walking around with a scowl or passionless gaze. As mentioned, you will have to turn off the smile when discussing serious issues. For example, Jimmy Carter went overboard with constant grinning during his 1976 presidential campaign. While it was initially refreshing, it got out of hand as it became a nervous mannerism. However, when speaking to an audience, regardless of size, your objective especially during the first 6 seconds is to bring the listeners closer - to pull them in, so to speak. A smile is the most efficient and credible method to achieve instant warmth.

Command Their Attention

Assuming the first 6 seconds have gone swimmingly, you now have 24 seconds to make your audience care about what you are going to say. There are several ways to grab the listeners' attention. One is to begin with a startling statistic. For example, if your subject is the marketing of pet food, you might begin with, "Recent visual test groups have reported that 90% of participants can't tell the difference between dog food and paté." Another is to share a personal anecdote: "I once had to rush a friend to the hospital because he thought a can of dog food in my refrigerator was chopped liver." Or, you may involve the audience right away: "How many of you think your pets care what their food looks like? Well the point is, you do. You've got to like what it looks like, because you're the one who buys it and serves it!" The idea is to get their attention. You can't wait and hope they eventually catch on. You must succeed in commanding their undivided focus immediately - there are no second chances to make a significant initial impact. Startling statistics, anecdotes (preferably personal) or audience-related questions practically guarantee immediate focus.

Now that you have their attention, you must convince the audience that by listening to you, there's something in it for them. They listen with vested self-interest, and unless you convince them right away that your message will benefit them, they will not respond. When you speak to people, no matter what the situation, they are usually sitting there thinking, "So what? Who cares? Why are you telling me this? Why should I want to listen? How will this information improve my life?"

In the first 30 seconds, you must take your audience past understanding to belief, from "I understand you, but who cares" to "I believe you because there's something here for me."

Establish Credibility

Credibility and executive presence go hand-in-hand. You're not credible to an audience if you don't take their needs into consideration - you're merely a "talking head." Announcing an objective that will benefit the listener will give you immediate credibility thus enhancing your executive presence.

Make your audience happier, smarter or richer!™ People want information they can use. In sales, a sales rep never talks features without stressing benefits, because he knows that features don't close the sale. If you were trying to sell a vacuum cleaner to a prospective client and you said yours was better and more powerful than any other cleaner on the market, it would probably sit there unsold. The question of what it will do for the customer was not answered.

But if you said yours will allow the customer to clean his house in half the time so he can have more minutes, even hours, to watch wrestling on TV - Bingo! - there's a benefit. A benefit is something that affects your audience personally, and they've got to hear it - something that's going to make them happier, smarter or richer - in the first 30 seconds!

+ People don't buy newspapers - they buy news
+ People don't buy books - they purchase knowledge and entertainment
+ People don't buy insurance - they acquire peace of mind
+ People don't buy homes - they obtain shelter and pride of ownership
+ People don't buy clothes - they select style

When you want to sell your boss on a new idea ask, "How will it make his/her life easier?" Think of benefits in terms of life being one continuous sales call. We are always selling something to people, whether we want them to come over for dinner, help us with a project, go to a certain resort on vacation or be convinced that we deserve a raise. You must try to offer your audience, prospects, and employers benefits in every conversation, and the most important time to do this is at the very beginning.

Be Interactive

It's also very important in the first 30 seconds to be interactive. *Telling* your audience is a great way to have information travel in one ear and out the other. But *showing* your audience, by selling in an interactive fashion, and odds are their brains will start to respond. Ask your audience a question (for example, "How many of you have ever thought about eating pet food?"), have someone stand up and share the stage with you (for example, "Tell us - what do you think a cat prefers for his lunch?"), anything to get their minds and bodies working. This will establish a high level of interest. They're not richer or smarter (yet), but they're definitely happier because you've engaged them.

Before the first 30 seconds are up, be sure you stop talking about yourself with pronouns like *I*, *me* and *my* and use more inclusive pronouns like *we*, *us* and *our*. You might think it's a small detail, but it really works and helps with audience buy-in. They will feel you care about them, and not just about yourself. Once again, your credibility is enhanced and so is your executive presence.

Think about it - who really wants to listen to a speaker go on and on about himself or herself? The speaker is there somehow to enhance the lives of the audience (make them happier, smarter, richer), not give a soliloquy. Jerry Seinfeld's comedic routines resonate so soundly with audiences because he always includes them in the jokes; it's always about "us," not just "him." And we laugh because we're in on it. So do tell an interesting story, and make sure we're included!

Primacy/Recency Effect™

This book discusses communication from a very unique perspective. To that end, I have developed a comprehensive series of axioms, rules, and mantras. I call them "Tamaraisms," and they are referenced throughout this book. There's also an appendix at the conclusion of "Be the Brand" which details each of them. The "Tamaraism" which most distinguishes my approach from my colleagues is a concept I call the **Primacy/Recency Effect - primacy** (primary) **equals first** and **recency** (most recent), **equals last**. *An audience remembers most what it hears first and last.* When discussing the first 30 seconds, an effective opening tells the audience precisely what you're planning to discuss, why they should care and your key points to support your point of view. It is crucial that you accomplish this at the very beginning.

Not long ago, at the request of a client, I attended an offsite meeting - you know, where a group gathers at a remote location, either a hotel or conference center, to discuss a project or crucial issues away from the distractions of the office. The individual who facilitated the meeting spent the first five minutes talking about the dinner they attended the evening before. He made a few jokes, dropped a harmless piece of gossip about the CEO, and discussed the enormity of the liquor bill. When he finally got to business, the attendees were deep in thought about how much each of them had drunk the previous evening and what jokes were made about them when they weren't in the room.

A week later, I was speaking to a group of those who had been at the offsite meeting, and to a person, all they could talk about was the inappropriate and distracting opening of the facilitator - and they remembered his remarks word for word!

Primacy/Recency tells us that what we say and do at the outset (and at the end) of any communication experience is of the utmost importance, and should be carefully crafted. I do not recommend memorizing presentations word-for-word. There are many pitfalls to this practice, including losing ones place, sounding 'canned' and always having to think about 'what's coming next'. However, I strongly recommend nailing two parts of your presentation - the opening and closing, which I repeat, the audience will remember most. What happens between the opening and closing will vary, depending upon your audience and other external factors. I call this **Outcome vs. Agenda**™ (another key "Tamaraism"), where the desired **outcome is fixed,** but the **agenda** (how you get to the outcome) **is fluid.** Linear speakers give the same presentations over and over again, exactly the same way and end up boring the heck out of the audience. The idea is to put yourself in the role of receivership and adjust accordingly. No two presentations should be exactly the same, but the desired outcome (the benefit to the audience) should never change - and we need to hear about it up front!!

Remember, there are no second chances when giving a presentation. The first 30 seconds are crucial. By looking ready, smiling, giving your audience something to care about and including them in the action, you will have gone a long way to ensure a successful communication experience.

The 30 Second Window of Opportunity
Test Yourself!

1. Within how many seconds does an audience decide whether or not they like how a speaker looks? When does the clock start ticking?

_____

2. Before you speak, what should every effective presenter do?

_____

3. What are three compelling ways to **grab your audience in the first 30 seconds**™?

_____

4. What is a benefit and why is it important to an audience?

_____

5. Why is it essential to be interactive?

_____

6. How do you make your language inclusive and why is it important?

_____

7. What is the **Primacy/Recency Effect?**

_____

8. What is meant by the phrase **Outcome vs. Agenda?**

_____

2

Personal Packaging™

"Style is the cutting edge of content."
Norman Mailer

MISSION STATEMENT
The medium for your message is the
way you present yourself.

You've surely heard the old saying, "It's not what's on the outside, but what's on the inside that counts." While we'd like to believe that's true, the harsh reality is that people remember us more for our style than for our substance. For instance:

+ John F. Kennedy, Jr., is remembered for his great smile and handsome, snappy Ivy League look.

+ Diana, Princess of Wales always looked chic in her superb clothing choices, and she interacted well with people regardless of socio-economic standing.

+ Cher seems perpetually youthful and wild, with off-beat clothing choices, always pushing the envelope.

+ Britney Spears focuses on body enhancement to minimize lack of performing skills.

+ Madonna, the Mistress of Reinvention, consistently changes her image with inconsistent choices - to great success!

+ Arnold Schwarzenegger is in evolution from body-builder/action hero to Armani icon.

Now, you *don't* have to wear Armani or be totally made-up every time you walk out your door, but if you want people to respond to your requests, part of the packaging secret is to put on your "game face." As presenters, we live in a fishbowl and are constantly being examined and judged. It's an unfortunate reality of life, and the better we deal with it, the more successful we'll become.

In the Bob Fosse biopic, *All That Jazz*, Roy Scheider - in his most memorable leading role - would always look in a mirror prior to a rehearsal, production or appearance, energize himself and say, "It's showtime!" This expression has become part of our lexicon. What it means for most of us is that it's now time to get up onstage, go on the air, appear before a crowd, address our staff, impress a potential date. It's always showtime when we interact with others. The spotlight is never turned off.

How do you feel when you walk down the street and pass someone who is dressed shabbily? If you're like most people, it probably makes you feel uncomfortable or superior in a self-conscious sort of way, right? We like to be around people who look good. It's been that way since the earliest days of man, from Hercules to Constantine to Elizabeth I to George Washington to Laura Bush.

We watch the *Oscars* or *Grammy Awards*, not so much for the ceremony, but to see how all the celebrities look. We love glancing at the supermarket tabloids on the checkout line for their columns on "Would you be caught dead in this outfit?" and for the best-dressed people of the week. We attend weddings and galas, not just to celebrate, but because being around well-dressed people makes us feel good. I'm not saying we should immediately stop running around town in sweats and tee shirts, but we should be strategic and remember that people make snap decisions based on our looks - and that's what they'll initially remember about you.

I learned this lesson when I moved from the anonymity of Manhattan to the intimacy of Princeton, NJ. I live on a fairly well-traveled street, and lots of commuters pass by my house during the early morning rush hour. This totally escaped me while putting out my trash one morning in my bathrobe and slippers. When I got to my office an hour later, there was a voicemail from one of my really important clients that said, "Saw you at the curb this morning... you with no make-up...not a pretty sight." I guess there's truth in jest! (Who would've known he was such an early riser?)

Why was the hit Bravo series *Queer Eye for the Straight Guy* so popular? Once you got beyond the conceit of five gay men "working on" a straight man, what it really boiled down to was that we loved seeing the end result of the makeover. When the clueless straight slob came out of his newly decorated bedroom with his new look and new duds, we were thrilled for him. I'll even go so far as to say that a substantial part of the straight male viewing audience wished the "Fab Five" had worked their magic on them!

Beyond *Queer Eye*, there have been and continue to be a huge number of makeover shows on cable and network television (some even involving plastic surgery). And they all focus on clothing as personal packaging, so let's talk about clothes.

To dress up or dress down…perhaps the biggest dilemma in corporate America is this hybrid term, "business casual." It's a major oxymoron. There's no such thing as casual clothes and sustained success, and I found this out the hard way. I was once asked to attend what's known as a "war games" session. It's a meeting where the client gathers all of their senior staff and brings in outside consultants to plot the advertising, public relations and general communication strategy for a particular product. The female president of the advertising agency charged with organizing this meeting was clearly wary of me, having known that I didn't think her agency was on track with the campaign they had put together. When I asked her what the dress code was going to be for the meeting, she replied, "You know the creative types in advertising. I guess you could call it funky casual." I believed her and dressed accordingly. The moment I arrived in my baggy dolman-sleeved sweater, corduroy pants and lace-up boots I knew I had been sandbagged. Everyone else arrived in their beautifully cut business suits with well-defined shoulders, while I appeared to shrink before their eyes in my "funky casual" outfit. I proceeded to cross my arms and legs the entire meeting, while trying to hide my unadorned and rather puny shoulders. My packaging was inappropriate, and I couldn't get over it or myself. The result was that I was self-conscious and sullen. The advertising agency went ahead with their flawed campaign, and I think I lost my client about $10 million that day!

Lesson learned - *it's better to overdress than underdress.* You can rarely go wrong if you're dressed more formally than your audience, but you can diminish yourself if you present a casual image to a more formal group.

I was able to put this to the test recently when a "hip" California company brought me in as a keynote speaker. I arrived as the only "suit" in a ubiquitous display of denim. But rather than making me feel uncomfortable, several members of the audience came up and apologized to me for what they perceived as their slide towards sloppiness. A flag for women in particular: don't call attention to body parts if you want to be credible. Thong underwear may be "in" right now, but we know when you're wearing it. Watch cleavage - too much and we're not sure just what you're trying to communicate. A blazer over anything squares you off and levels the playing field! It's versatile and adds instant stature. It's also *removable*. However, that doesn't work in reverse; if you didn't bring it, you can't manufacture it on the spot. Plan your wardrobe accordingly if you're looking to impress with a more executive presence.

Yes, Colors Do Count!

I'm not a big believer in that color/season fad that was so popular in the early 1990s. It created stereotypes, and I personally didn't want to go around the rest of my life with the label of "winter type." Winter can be very gloomy, yet for a while, I bought into it. I was persuaded to buy only blacks and grays and allowed to add only small splashes of color. When I look back at my early videotaped seminars, it seems like I was wearing a uniform - shades of Hillary Clinton and her black pants suits! I was awash in a sea of soot. I now own an array of colors and pull them out as the mood and occasion demand; blue is most popular, red energetic, yellow cheerful, white crisp, brown calming and black authoritative.

When Senator Bob Dole ran for President in 1996, his most effective campaigner was his wife Elizabeth - now a U.S. senator from North Carolina. When she made her historic keynote address at the '96 Republican National

Convention (remember her leaving the podium to go out into the audience?…
more on effective movement later), her entrance music was *My Guy* - with the
appropriate lyrics, "I got sunshine, on a cloudy day!" and she strategically wore
a bright yellow skirt suit. While her husband did not do well at the polls, her
successful "sunny" appearance helped propel her into elective office some years
later. Interestingly enough, Hillary Clinton (who, when not wearing black
seemed married to pale blue), introduced former President Bill Clinton at the
2004 Democratic National Convention wearing a (guess what) bright yellow
pantsuit! Clearly, Hillary was borrowing a page from Liddy Dole's playbook,
and lots of thought went into choosing this uplifting, *sunny* wardrobe color.

Teresa Heinz Kerry made some bold color choices during the 2004 presidential campaign - rich burgundy, red, navy, delft blue, taupe - which corresponded
with her bold personality. She rarely wore the same color in the same week.
The variety made her appearances more memorable. (Positive or negative, she
got much more press than Laura Bush!)

Men generally look authoritative in a dark suit and can lighten up their appearance with a pastel shirt and colorful tie (notice how politicians always seem to
be wearing a red tie! In warm weather, light color suits and sport coats - khaki,
olive, cream - can be quite dashing, especially when worn with "summery" pink,
yellow, and light blue shirts. (Pink has become the new neutral.) Men and
women both need to steer clear of stark white shirts, suits or dresses because
they reflect light and can be a distraction. Off-white or cream works better.

I part company with the fashion experts who declare that heavyset people
should stick to dark colors. Color is not partial to body type, and heavier

men and women can look great in rich, colorful clothing, appropriate to their skin tone. Where larger-bodied people need to be careful is in the selection of patterns. Bold patterns on big people simply do not work (unless you're auditioning for the next revival of *Guys and Dolls*).

Put Patterns in Their Place

An esteemed food critic once told me that it's hard to eat an impressive meal off a busy plate - the design hurts your digestion, and a pattern confuses the palette. If you want to distract people from what you have to say, then a multitude of conflicting checks, stripes and plaids will certainly do the trick. Stick to solids with splashes of color and patterns. Remember - a little goes a long way. The bigger the body, the smaller (and therefore tighter) the pattern should be. When we recall the image of Jackie Onassis, Audrey Hepburn, the Duke of Windsor, or currently, *Today* show host, Matt Lauer - understated elegance comes to mind. This can be a guide to you when choosing patterns.

"Peek-A-Boo" - Make Sure They Can't See You!

My mentor, Larry P., the former president of a large company, taught me a very important lesson about clothing. I share it with you because it had a major impact on someone's career, and the same could happen to you.

Larry was a stickler for personal packaging. Every night before he went to bed, he studied his schedule for the following day and laid out his wardrobe to fit what he'd be doing. This was not to save him time the next morning, but rather to strategize for his various meetings in order to maximize his effect. This attention to detail has helped propel him to tremendous success in his field.

Larry was in the process of hiring a new vice president for marketing and was considering promoting an individual from within the company. He had a candidate whose credentials and experience were superb, but with one major problem - his personal packaging was poor. His clothing was careless, faded and cheap-looking. He also did not wear tee shirts and his see-through poly-fiber shirts allowed us a birds-eye view of his rather hairy upper torso, which was most unflattering. Larry could not have an executive on his team who presented himself like that. So I was brought in to help this candidate purchase some new clothing and put together an executive look.

We went to Barney's, the iconic men's fashion emporium, and I must say, I did a good job of selecting some new suits, shirts, tee shirts, ties, slacks, shoes and socks. He looked a lot better. But soon he began to mix his new clothing with his old. He did not take care of his wardrobe. The tee shirts (when he wore them) became yellow. He reverted to his former disheveled self while thinking he looked just fine. "Peek-A-Boo" Man, as I called him, did not get the job.

Snappy dressing will not guarantee you the corner office and an executive position, but I can say with great authority that poor dressing can be a serious impediment to progressing in one's chosen career. The previous chapter on the first 30 seconds demonstrates that you don't have a second chance to make a first impression. This not only applies to meetings and formal presentations but to other initial communication venues, such as job interviews. Prior to any interview it's imperative that you investigate the company's dress culture. Recently, I was brought in to do some executive coaching with an employee at a well-known financial institution. During our time together, an account supervisor who was hoping to be promoted to a managerial position came by for an interview with my client. She took one look at him in the waiting area and told me that there was no way he was getting the job. I thought he looked pretty snappy. He had on a nice dark suit with a light purple shirt and coordinated tie. My client hated the shirt and felt that the bank would be poorly represented by this image. She went through the motions of an interview with this young man, but he was immediately eliminated from consideration. You might say that my client was too harsh in her judgment. However, the bottom line is that the man did not get the job. Had he done a little homework to find out what his interviewer's more conservative preferences were, he might have garnered the position. Interviewers look for reasons to reject applicants. Don't give them a chance with inappropriate attire.

Accessories

Accessories are essential, and in the context of today's lifestyle they matter even more! The Nike running shoe, the Coach briefcase, the Concord watch - they all take on more importance. A brilliant clothing designer once told me that if I couldn't afford anything else, I should buy at least one piece of expensive leather: a briefcase, belt, purse or pair of shoes. He said it's hard to look insignificant when you're carrying a Fendi bag or wearing Prada shoes. Think of your business clothing as an investment. You will always be better off with a few high-end ensembles as opposed to a wide variety of inexpensive pieces. Premium clothing fits better, wears better, looks better, and is cheaper in the long run because it has to be replaced less often. Men should be very careful when selecting neckties. A cheap tie can sink an expensive suit, while an elegant tie can raise the bar on a more modest ensemble. The same goes for shoes. Cheap shoes are not only bad for your feet but look shoddy, even from a distance. Just how seriously should you take fashion? I don't often misstep (no pun intended) when I give feedback. I'm very aware that I'm dealing with a person's self-image and ego. However, recently I was working with a group of what this company called their "high potential" sales professionals. For the most part, they were all appropriately dressed in their best business attire, with the exception of one glaring outlier. She had on a tan pantsuit, orange shell and shocking tangerine shoes. She felt really coordinated. The problem was that the shoes were extremely pointed and very spiked, at least five inches high. When I suggested that they caused us to look at her feet (instead of her face, for example), she proudly proclaimed, "Yes, I'm known for my tangerine shoes." Think about it - is that really going to enhance her credibility and drive sales?

I serve as a guest speaker for an extremely impressive "Women in Leadership" program at a very old and very famous single-sex college. The young women in this program are intensely serious about their executive presence. Recently, after delivering a keynote address to this earnest group of aspiring professionals (who were all asked to wear business attire to the event), they each came up to shake my hand. One by one, they introduced themselves and even gave me their business cards. I had been admiring the wonderful "buttoned-down" appearance of a girl in the second row until later, when she was standing in front of me, I looked down and saw she was wearing sparkling silver lamé pumps. Clearly, she still had some work to do.

Above all, your packaging should not distract from your message. Though it's currently very fashionable, women should avoid big, clunky jewelry or bracelets and necklaces that jiggle because these take focus. (And if you're using a microphone, the resonance of the clattering jewelry will sound like rattlesnakes throughout the room!) Straight, curly, short or long, your hair should be in place and off your face so you're not continually tucking it behind your ears. Men should take it easy on the hair gel, eliminate worn items (you know those belt buckles that started out gold and are quickly fading to silver) and make sure everything you're wearing fits well. If you can't button the jacket, don't wear it. If your pleats don't lie flat and spread when you button your trousers, don't wear them! Heavier men should avoid pleats altogether.

Men and women - take it easy on the scents. We don't want to smell your cologne or perfume after you've left the room. The rule of thumb is - if you're not close enough for your audience to kiss you, and they can smell your scent - then you're wearing too much!

While this all may seem like common sense, you'd be amazed how many people make grave errors because they think no one will notice. The truth is that we notice everything - and everybody is looking, all the time. In the theatre, a common error of performers is to check out the audience from the wings. They assume the audience is focused on the stage and won't notice them. The reality is that if you can see the audience, they can see you! You're never offstage, even if someone else is speaking or you're not in the spotlight.

Just as important as preparing and rehearsing your presentation is attention to your personal packaging. Before you leave your home or office, check yourself out in the mirror - from top to bottom. Make sure you like what you see. If you don't, chances are your audience won't either. If you do, you're sure to project a more confident and commanding presence.

Personal Packaging
Test Yourself!

1. What is meant by "Game Face"?

   _____

2. Why is "business casual" considered an oxymoron?

   _____

3. What are the dangers of being underdressed? Overdressed?

   _____

4. What should guide your color choices?

   _____

5. What clothing and accessory choices are distracting?

   _____

6. What's the rule regarding perfume and cologne?

   _____

CHAPTER 2

3

Body Language

"Our body is a machine for living."
Leo Tolstoy

MISSION STATEMENT
Light travels faster than sound; we see things before we hear
them. Your body language is the vessel for your message.

Consider the following:

+ In 1960, the stiff, aggressive Richard Nixon lost the presidential race to John F. Kennedy, who was so good-looking and at ease with himself. Chalk that win up to body language.

+ In 1980, the folksy Ronald Reagan ("there you go again") beat Jimmy Carter, who as president had evolved to an image of serious and angry. Body language again.

+ In 1992, George H.W. Bush's hand gestures and darting eyes were seemingly out of control (fodder for SNL comedian Dana Carvey) while Arkansas governor, Bill Clinton, was a relaxed, charismatic man of the people who appeared to know how to interact with all of us.

+ In 1996 and 2000 George Jr., while not exactly charismatic (facial grimaces aside) looked positively animated when compared to stiff Al Gore, and four years later to, if possible, a stiffer John Kerry.

Leverage Body Language™

Meeting with a teacher at a school conference, sitting on the sidelines at a soccer game among other parents, greeting a blind date - even waving to someone we know - all require us to step out of our shell and put on our best face. People's impressions of you are based on these interactions.

Professor Albert Mehrabian's famous UCLA interpersonal communication study, which has become the gold standard in my industry, tells us that only 7% of message retention comes from content and 38% from vocal use - tone and pitch. This leaves 55% for appearance and body language!

Over half of our communication retention is transmitted through our bodies - the rest is through words. Could this be because sometimes your mouth is saying one thing while your body is saying something completely different? In addition, swaying back and forth, picking at clothing, scratching and other nervous habits distract and take away from your message. The fact is, whether you're standing in the back of a room during a meeting, walking up from the audience to come to the podium for a speech or passing a co-worker in the hall, you are communicating every step of the way - *with body language!*

People say things with their eyes, mouth, neck, shoulders, back, arms, legs and overall body posture. And we definitely take notice! Dick Van Dyke is a perfect example of a man who has aged gracefully, from agile young TV comedy writer Rob Petrie on *The Dick Van Dyke Show* in the 1960s to the respected and distinguished doctor/detective, Dr. Mark Sloane, on *Diagnosis Murder* in the 1990s. But what we probably remember about him, to this day, is the way he used his body, whether it was dancing on rooftops to *Chim, Chim Cheree* in

Mary Poppins or humorously falling over the ottoman at the opening of *The Dick Van Dyke Show.*

Your body (face, arms, legs and torso) can do some amazing things, and people will remember you not only for what you say, but how you say it! Do we need an incredibly agile body like Dick Van Dyke's to communicate? Not at all.

Let's take, for example, the late actor/writer/director Christopher Reeve who was an inspiration in the way he remained positive after his tragic 1994 riding accident that left him paralyzed. I had the opportunity to work with one of Mr. Reeve's personal physicians on a potential media campaign. I noticed the ease with which he spoke to reporters, his passion, his "laser" eye contact with everyone he encountered. This prominent doctor told me he learned how to connect by watching his famous patient. "He had 90% of his body movement gone and nothing to work with but his face and voice, yet he learned how to reposition his head slightly when he disagreed with you and how to put his face forward to make a point. He used frowns, smiles, furrowed brows, lots of slight nuances to make points - and he did! Everything was so subtle, but so calculated."

Christopher Reeve's body language, even on such a limited basis, was used brilliantly. This high profile physician now imitates some things he learned from his famous patient, implementing them, using them very effectively in interviews, which is quite amazing. It's not every day you hear about a doctor *learning* from his patient!

As a young actor, even before he blazed across the screen as "Superman," Chris Reeve was taught that stage presence isn't a trait we are born with - it's something we must learn to use. But how?

In his book *Unlimited Power*, "peak performance expert" Anthony Robbins says that physiology is the "lever to emotional change." We may think of depression as an emotional state, he says, but we view it as a physical one. Think about the body language of someone who is feeling sorry for himself - his gaze is downward, he's unsmiling, his shoulders are slumped.

Compare that to the person who appears to be happy, full of energy and verve; posture erect, her eyes and mouth are inviting. This is the person I want you to be in your presentation. Even if you think it's an act, your audience won't because this is the person who exhibits charisma. I'm sure there are plenty of happy people with bad posture and unsmiling faces as well as depressed people standing tall with sunny faces. But in presentations, *we're dealing with perceptions*. An audience is not able or willing to take the time to dig beneath the surface to determine "how you really feel." What they see (what you telegraph) is what they get.

One can only imagine the emotional toll that the Monica Lewinsky scandal took on Bill Clinton. However, a few days after the story broke, President Clinton was scheduled to give the annual State of the Union address. Talk about bad timing! Clinton's aides strongly urged him to postpone the address. They figured that everyone would be thinking about him and Monica (remember the endless rerunning of the video of Ms. Lewinsky wearing her funny hat, hugging the President), and not listening to what he had to say. Clinton, being the master communicator, had a smarter take on the situation. He would give the address as scheduled. He would not hide and appear contrite. He would (remember, the State of the Union is televised) be commanding, confident and in control. He felt (rightly so) that his demeanor would say more to the American people than any words he would utter that night.

From the very moment the sergeant-at-arms announced his arrival at the joint session of Congress, Clinton was the model of a commander-in-chief. His smiling, warm countenance reached out to congressmen on both sides of the aisle. He stood tall before the Senate and House of Representatives and spoke with strength and eloquence. Not many people remember what was said in his address that evening, but we remember his smiling, strong, and determined demeanor. Only he knows the depths of the personal despair he may have been feeling, but that is exactly the opposite of what he wanted the American people to see, and it was highly successful!

San Francisco University researcher Dr. Paul Ekman put it bluntly: "We are what we show on our faces. To change your state, alter your posture. If you want to look and feel good, start smiling, even if you don't feel like it, and your attitude will soon change. This will trigger biological processes, like increased blood flow and oxygen to the brain and the mind's perception of how the human is supposed to feel will change." That's what actors do so well. They're always wearing somebody else's face and body, switching brilliantly to become that persona (like Robert DeNiro in such diverse films as *Taxi Driver*, *Raging Bull*, *The Deer Hunter* and *The Untouchables*).

I've heard time and time again that in order to ease nerves and appear relaxed, speakers should visualize everyone in the audience wearing only their underwear. Yuck - what a ghastly thought! What you should do is pretend that the audience is the mirror and see yourself in their eyes, looking terrific! The mythical Princess Fiona didn't fall in love with Shrek because he looked at her with fear and self-disgust. Fiona saw the love and devotion in his eyes, which made the ogre look noble and princely!

The Eyes Have It!™

I have a friend who discovered a relative in the Ukraine, by way of the Internet. They exchanged pictures, but unfortunately my American friend was wearing sunglasses, making the photo useless to his newly found cousin Galina.

"The eyes are everything," she wrote to him in an email. "In our country, eyes are the windows to the soul. Nothing else matters." While it's not so dramatic here in America (although it's curious that mobsters are often photographed wearing sunglasses), eye contact is certainly vital to being an effective communicator. It was the poet Ralph Waldo Emerson who wrote that, "Eyes can threaten like a loaded pistol, insult like a hiss or kick or by beams of kindness make the heart dance with joy." It makes sense, doesn't it? In the silent films of the early 20th century - it was all about the expression of the eyes. With one look, Rudolph Valentino could bring a theatre full of women to their knees. When you communicate with someone, do you look at his or her mouth, nose or eyes? I'm pretty certain you chose number three. Eyes are our vehicles of choice for personal interactions.

The late Diana, Princess of Wales, used eye contact to brilliantly overcome her shyness. When she first became part of the royal family, her nervous demeanor was clear as she looked down at the ground and shrugged her shoulders. Over time, however, she became a master at connecting with people instantly. This was not genius. She merely learned that her job was to look people in the eye and make them feel important. People read your face while reacting to your body.

When speaking to large groups, it's impossible to look everyone in the eye when you speak to them (unless you're a fly with hundreds of little eyes!). However, the idea is to connect with as many people as possible throughout your presentation. An acronym commonly used in my business addresses this issue: **S.T.O.P.** - **S**ingle **T**hought, **O**ne **P**erson™. What this basically means is that in any size group, you can think of a section of the room as a person. Make eye contact with that section while communicating a single thought. When you've completed the thought, you indicate a transition either by taking a step or two or by changing your focus to another section, and then you communicate your next thought. This method not only allows you to effectively make eye contact and connect with your audience, it also communicates when a thought is finished and a new thought is begun. It also eliminates the dreaded "security camera effect" that plagues many speakers who feel they have to make eye contact with everyone in the audience by sweeping their head back and forth across the room at regular intervals.

Light Travels Faster Than Sound

While I devote a later chapter to effective movement, it's important to mention movement and gesturing here, in the context of body language. *We **see** you before we **hear** you.* When you do move, it should be with confidence and energy. Good posture is a prerequisite. People who stroll with hunched-over shoulders and shuffle along slowly are people we generally don't want to be around. Most successful people move with authority by holding their chests out, shoulders back and stomachs in. You should too, from the very beginning - remember the all-important first 6 seconds!.

Nervous energy has to go somewhere, but I'm not a big advocate of unfinished or endlessly repetitive hand gestures. The appropriate use of hands can be very effective (remember, we see you before we hear you, and hands can underscore your message), but inappropriate gesturing can be distracting. As I've said, former President George H.W. Bush is a perfect example of gestures that should have been reeled in. Dana Carvey was merciless in his impression. His hands were out like flippers. Gestures must have a beginning, a middle and an end. The beginning is your "at rest", the middle is the actual gesture, and the end is the return to the "at rest" position. What did you want to say to George? "Put them away, Mr. President!" In more recent years, Vice President Dick Cheney has become regular fodder for Jon Stewart and Stephen Colbert, for, among other things, his *lack* of gestures or much movement of any kind when speaking.

We gesture for a number of reasons. First of all, gesturing gets us energized and makes us more expressive. In a way, we are almost acting like musical conductors with our voices as our gestures reflect changes in pitch, rhythm, energy and volume. Gesturing also burns off nervous energy, but you've got to be careful about what you do with your hands when you're in front of a group. For example, I know if I put my hands behind my back, I start conducting with my head and begin to look like a pigeon pecking for his lunch. My energy has to find an outlet, and for me apparently my outlet is my head.

One of former California Governor Gray Davis's problems (he had so many) was his hand gestures. While vainly struggling to hold onto office against Arnold Schwarzenegger's onslaught, he tried to give the thumbs up sign to his audiences. However, he couldn't even do that well, and somehow his thumb always went sideways - not a good omen. During the 2004 presidential campaign, Sen. John Kerry was a fan of holding up his fists, but instead of closing his fist with his thumb, he placed his thumb on the side against his index finger, so it looked almost dainty and unconvincing. It also looked contrived, which was and remains an all-around communication issue for Senator Kerry.

My husband likes to hold his hands behind his back when he speaks. I call it "the firing squad stance." Other gestures I find questionable are crossing your arms on your chest which looks condescending (remember your 3rd grade teacher?) or folding your hands at crotch level (the fig leaf stance). I prefer what I call the "ready position", with one hand placed loosely inside the other, knees slightly flexed and ready to move, so you can go right or left. You won't lose your balance and you'll be able to stand up for an hour and not be tired.

Remember, to get audiences to focus on the presentation, control your mannerisms. You know a speaker is bombing when you see him playing with his hair, grabbing and tapping a pen, coughing nervously or clearing his throat a lot. These distractions are what people will remember about you - not the information, but rather the way you delivered it.

Those Dreaded Pockets

I work with a corporate CEO who's a brilliant speaker, but it has taken me years to get him to stop putting his hands in his pockets when he speaks. This is generally a problem for men (women's clothing is usually devoid of pockets). The speaker is nervous and doesn't know what to do with his hands, so he "finds home" and shoves them in his pockets. But all that nervous energy has to manifest itself somehow. So, those in-pocket hands start shaking the change (*Jingle Bells* anyone?) and rummaging around (maybe searching for old receipts?), and pretty soon, *all* we're focusing on is that busy hand activity going on at pelvis level.

When was the last time you saw a really great speaker stand onstage for an hour with his hands in his pockets? Probably never. The hand-in-the-pocket-while-speaking syndrome was such a problem for one well-known Chicago attorney that he had 35 suits custom tailored with no pants pockets, just to make sure that his hands couldn't "find home" in them. It was an expensive method to say the least, but one worth considering if that is what it takes to keep your hands where they're supposed to be - bent slightly at the biggest knuckle close to your body, at the ready position, in place for those expensive gestures which support your message so well.

Take the Stage!

Back in Michigan when I was first starting out, a must experience for all those who were considering any career that involved public speaking was the Montgomery Ward Charm School. I kid you not. They told us how to speak, how to stand, how to carry ourselves, how to "e-nun-ci-ate," etc.

At any rate, one of the great insights imparted by this program was that a woman, when standing in front of a group, should stand slightly sideways with her body at an angle, arms close to her sides. This would create a more "feminine presence." "Feminine presence" was a code phrase for "look as thin as possible." Well, that's what I did, and guess what? I looked really thin - and really insignificant.

While women are told at an early age that they should take up as little space as possible, the plain truth is that turning sideways and angling your body makes you look weak and unassuming. I've seen so many women (men don't seem to do this) practically disappear in front of groups in a desperate effort to "look thin." Don't succumb to this! Face forward with your legs positioned at the same width as your shoulders, slightly flexed, and don't be afraid to extend your arms as far as you need to when making gestures. As they say in the theatre, "Take the stage!" While some may feel that being "thin" is flattering, it's a surefire way to make you - and your message - disappear.

Body Language
Test Yourself!

1. What percentage of message retention is affected by body language?

   _____

2. Exactly, how does body language communicate?

   _____

3. Why is perception more significant than reality?

   _____

4. What part of the face expresses the most?

   _____

5. What's the most effective way to make eye contact with a large group?

   _____

6. Describe effective gesturing and ineffective gesturing.

   _____

7. What are the dangers of "hands in pockets"?

   _____

8. What is meant by "Take the Stage"?

4

V.E.I.M. - Vocal Excellence is Mandatory™

"There is no index of character as sure as the voice."
Benjamin Disraeli

MISSION STATEMENT
The right vocal delivery can sell your points; the wrong
delivery can stop them dead in their tracks.

A bland, disconnected vocal quality shows us you don't care - enthusiasm and an animated voice is what we all prefer to hear. Think of Oprah Winfrey versus Queen Elizabeth II of England. Everyone who has met Her Majesty says she's a lovely person, but the only reason most people listen to her speeches is because they have to - she's the queen! I've seen her put Parliament to sleep on BBC with her mezzo drone and total lack of vocal inflection.

It may not be your goal to whip your audience into a frenzy all the time, but you certainly don't want to put them to sleep. So, let's talk about vocal skills: speaking loudly with a varied rate, appropriate pitch placement, good phrasing, frequent pauses and an efficient breathing style.

I break down verbal communication into components called paralanguage elements. They include:

+ **Breathing:** This one act does so much more than provide the oxygen we need to live. It also greatly affects the sound and rhythm of our voices. I call it the trampoline for all vocal gymnastics.

- **Weight:** This is the energy in your voice.
- **Rate:** Listeners' comprehension and retention of your message is dependent upon how fast (or slow) you speak. Energized is best.
- **Pause:** This is the equivalent of vocal punctuation marks for your sentences.
- **Volume:** Can people hear you? Are you too loud?
- **Pitch:** Our vocal cords are capable of producing a spoken pitch range of 12 to 14 notes.
- **Inflection/Word Stress - Variety/Personalization:** Most people don't totally "flatline" when they speak (Henry Kissinger being a major exception to this; I'll never understand how he rated so highly with so many women!). To get the point across, we bend and stress key words and phrases.

Each paralanguage component represents a different, but necessary, element of effective speech. I will now discuss each one in more detail to demonstrate how they affect your vocal production.

Breathing

Frank Sinatra, universally considered one of the greatest vocalists of the 20th century, identified breathing as a major key to his success. Sinatra's easygoing style always appeared effortless; he would just open his mouth and the songs came out. However, as with most outstanding artists, this innate skill was the result of a great deal of concentrated work and practice.

As the featured singer for band leader Tommy Dorsey's orchestra in the 1940s, Sinatra noticed that Dorsey could hold the notes on his trombone for as long as an amazing 16 measures (over half a minute!) without a break. Sinatra wanted to apply that same sort of breath control to his singing, as a way to stand out from the crowd. And he methodically set out to become a breath master.

"I began swimming in public pools, taking laps underwater and thinking song lyrics to myself as I swam," Sinatra told an interviewer. The effort paid off - he was soon singing up to 8 measures without taking a break, compared to other singers who could only manage 2 to 4 bars. Sinatra's lyrics seemed to have a better rhythm to them, and soon, bobby-soxers across America were swooning over the young crooner from Hoboken, New Jersey. He was soon able to quit the Dorsey band and go solo - all thanks in large part to his breathing technique.

Now I'm not saying that if you adjust your breathing, you'll have swarms of screaming fans lining up to hear you, but it will certainly have a major impact on the success or failure of your oral presentation. *Where and when you breathe determines how you sound.* Stand up for a minute and put your hands on your clavicle. This is what people do when they're nervous - they raise their shoulders and direct their breath into their throats - and they sound much like President George W. Bush when asked about the governments plan for rebuilding New Orleans right after Hurricane Katrina.

The best type of breathing is diaphragmatic. Don't take a proper diaphragmatic breath and your voice will sound distorted, often shaky and insecure, like a teenage boy during a voice change. Take fewer, deeper breaths and you'll have a stronger vocal presence. You'll feel more relaxed and your voice will sound more relaxed. *Before you utter a word at the beginning of any presentation, a deep, diaphragmatic breath is mandatory.*

Weight

Here's an exercise to try: Put both hands on your rib cage about waist high. Now take in a slow deep breath. As you do, you should feel your rib cage expand. Count slowly to seven while keeping your rib cage expanded. The secret here is a stingy outflow of breath, which should be sustained until the end of the 7th count. Repeat this routine several times. You must fight the urge to collapse. Get used to this type of breathing. Congratulations - you've just created *phrasing!* You're now speaking with controlled breath, something I call "meaning clusters."

After breath, weight is the single most important element of the paralanguage equation. If you don't sound energized, you won't sound committed. And if you don't care about what you're saying, no one else will either.

How to do that? The simplest way is by acting like we're speaking to young children. That is when we are most comfortable, animated and natural. We can't assume an interest level. Little children aren't yet schooled in the area of being polite, and they will tune you out unless you make a real effort. So what do you do? You become more animated and interesting!

This is not to say that you should speak during a presentation as if you're addressing a group of 3-year-olds. The feeling of being patronized is a major turnoff. However, just as you cannot assume an interest level with children, you cannot assume your audience shares the same interest level - or familiarity with your topic - as you do. You must always speak as if your audience is hearing your words for the very first time. Think back to the last time you told a joke. Didn't you find that you were much more animated than during regular conversation? And when you got to the punch line, wasn't it even more ener-gized and weighted because you wanted to make sure it was heard and under-stood? The same holds true for your presentation. The more animated and energized your speech, the greater the odds that your message will be heard, understood and appreciated.

Rate

One of the many businesses for which I have consulted on media issues is a well-known pharmaceutical company that recently merged. They marketed such diverse prescription products as anti-fungal and pain management drug therapies. Vocal rate became a major issue for their presenters at a press con-ference where they introduced the company's new blockbuster medication. These executives rarely met with the media, but since they were experienc-ing some stiff competition from another major drug manufacturer in the same field, they decided they needed to get their message out to the press, as well as Wall Street analysts, in a timely manner.

I coached the company's executives before the session and reminded them to be engaging and, most importantly, speak with energy. We seemed to be in synch until the dress rehearsal when these executives, who had, up to that point, been so good in their previous rehearsals, suddenly began to act like zombies, speaking really slowly and putting us all to sleep.

How could this have happened, I wondered? Did they all take one of their patented sedatives? Furious, I began pacing the room and noticed that on the back of the execs' name cards at each head table were four words handwritten in large letters: SPEAK SLOWLY AND DISTINCTLY.

It turned out that the office administrative assistant had written these instructions, thinking she was helping, when in fact she was potentially destroying the entire session! I quickly "thanked" her for the "help," reminded my clients how they were supposed to speak, got out a magic marker and blacked out the back of the cards. Luckily, the day was saved before the press and analysts arrived.

"Speak slowly and distinctly" is a common misconception. If you do that today, you're dead. Slowly and distinctly is worse than fast and hysterical - at least if you're fast, you have energy going somewhere. If you speak slowly with everything suppressed, your audience won't care because you'll be putting them to sleep. Energy is needed to keep the audience's attention.

The average rate of speech for most people is about 150-175 words per minute. This may sound like a lot, but keep in mind that the human brain can process about 600 words per minute! Does this mean that you have to speak like an auctioneer trying to coax bids out of a reluctant crowd at a charity benefit? Not necessarily. Most people would lose what you were saying. Even though the brain is capable of processing the words, the mind rejects most of it if too much information comes at it all at once. However, I can't tell you how many times I've listened to speakers with a slow rate and found myself mentally finishing all of their sentences before they did. My mind is telling me that I wish they'd get on with it. It's deadening and, quite frankly, annoying.

So, in our perfect world, don't speak too slowly and do speak with energy - fast enough to keep your audience engaged but not so fast that you trip over what you are trying to say.

Pause Power™

As a rapid speaker, I'm a big user of pauses. I use them for mental ventilation and to create verbal punctuation. The pause says to the listener, "What I just said is important. I'm going to allow some time to let it sink in."

Most speakers avoid pauses for two reasons. One, they're afraid of forgetting a piece of information or not being able to fit everything in. They have to keep barreling ahead with no breaks. Another is that they're deathly afraid of any silence; they think every nanosecond needs to be filled with sound as though a pause will appear as if they've forgotten what they're supposed to be saying. To the first reason, I say that pauses need to be planned - they are to be used for very specific purposes. Pauses should be an integral part of your presentation technique, not an ad-hoc interruption that throws you. They should also take very little cumulative time. To the second reason, I say quite simply that every now and then, dead air is good! A pause refreshes, emphasizes and permits reflection. And even if you do forget something and take a pause to get your bearings, the audience doesn't know that (unless you tell them, of course).

Pauses are also a great interviewing technique. I used them often and to great effect when I was a television reporter. Apparently, I was in very good company. Larry King and Barbara Walters have both been quoted as saying that when they ask a question and someone doesn't immediately answer, they just pause and stare back at them. The pause makes the interviewee realize that he or she is expected to say more and start to "dish."

The great comedian, Jack Benny, created a character who was cheap, played the violin poorly and used long blank stares to make a point. He was known for his effective use of pausing to achieve his greatest laughs. "It's not so much knowing when to speak," Benny said about his comedy, "as when to pause."

Classic Benny:
A robber walks up to Benny, puts a gun to his back and says,
"Your money or your life!"
Silence.
"Well, what's it going to be?"
More silence.
"I'm thinking…" says Benny. "I'm thinking."

This routine, punctuated by Benny's long pause, got one of the biggest laughs of his career when it was first performed on radio in the 1930s and later on television in the 1960s.

The power of the pause isn't exactly a new concept. It harkens all the way back to the days of Homer. In the *Iliad*, the narrator comments on the pause by writing, "Persuasive speech, and more persuasive sighs, silence that spoke and eloquence of eyes."

One person with whom we associate pause overuse is the hammy Captain Kirk of the "Starship Enterprise" in *Star Trek*; William Shatner. He boldly went where no other actor dreamed to go in terms of delivery. His "Beam… Me… Up… Scotty… Right now!" became fodder for comedians who could imitate him with ease. As spokesperson for Priceline.com, he parodies himself with his pause-laden camera-leering and heavy-duty takes. He also uses these trademarks on *Boston Legal* and his cable reality show.

However, a major public figure who became the master of the effective pause is Colin Powell. Listen carefully next time you have the opportunity to hear him speak. His delivery is crisp, varied and extremely image-laden. In order for those images to sink in, he punctuates his phrases with many pauses, with tremendous success. Since he retired as Secretary of State he is back out on the speaker circuit (raking in the big bucks) topped only by Rudy Giuliani and Bill Clinton.

Another powerful pauser is (surprise!) Bill Clinton - currently the highest paid professional speaker on the circuit. He has a clever way to fill pauses - he animates them! Remember when he was being deposed by the U.S. Senate subcommittee ("It depends on what is is ...)? He used those up-palm gestures, crossing and uncrossing his fingers, all the while maintaining eye contact with his inquisitors. The result? They stayed connected and so did you. He sometimes bought himself as much as seven seconds before he arrived at a thoughtful next statement or response. More recently, in the 2004 series of presidential debates, John Kerry successfully used the same technique (it even has a name, the Von Rostoff Effect). While he did not win the election, following the debates Senator Kerry's numbers shot up and dramatically narrowed the gap between him and President Bush. Animated pauses not only buy time, they set up what you're about to say.

Before your next presentation, think carefully about how you can use pauses to make your speech patterns more forceful and effective.

Volume

When stage actors begin their careers, they are encouraged to follow in the foot-steps of stars with big booming voices such as the late Ethel Merman (*Gypsy, Annie Get Your Gun, Anything Goes*) who could fill up large theatres with her clarion voice, without the aid of amplification. Well, times have changed, and today we have all sorts of sophisticated amplification equipment, so even those with smaller voices shouldn't have a problem being heard.

However, "just being heard" is not necessarily the goal of an effective speaker. A more energetic tone will make sure that your words seem more powerful and authoritative. Even more effective is to vary the volume of your voice for emphasis. Louder usually means "Now get this!" It can work the other way as well. Speaking softly, with energy, also gets our attention. The old broker-age firm, E.F. Hutton, created a whole advertising campaign around a variety of situations (restaurants, meetings, gatherings) when individuals whispered to one another, "My broker at E.F. Hutton told me ..." and everyone else in the room stopped and leaned in to overhear. The voice-over in a hushed tone would then pronounce, "When E.F. Hutton speaks... everyone listens." This created a whole mentality of speaking softly to create an image of power.

However you use it, volume can be a significant method of communicating key points and guaranteeing attention.

Pitch

Pop divas such as Mariah Carey and classical artists such as Renee Flemming aren't just recognized for their pleasing vocal styles but also for the mastery of their crafts; they can produce 2, 3 and sometimes nearly 4 octaves of notes.

Most of us, however, utilize a speaking range of less than one octave, mostly because we don't know any better. Personally, I wasn't made aware of this until I began working with a high-priced New York vocal coach who encouraged me to hit a broader range of notes as a way to keep the audience's interest. It was an expensive lesson that I now pass on to you.

In discussing the perfect pitch - what we call "optimum" - you don't want to be too high or too low, but right in the middle as a baseline for vocal variation. Think of it as speaking in the key that works best for you.

Try the following: vocalize the sound "eeeee" on a sustained breath in a downward sequence until your voice begins to crackle. Now, reverse your pitch upward until your voice finds a very obvious place at which it suddenly becomes louder. Congratulations! You have now found your *optimum pitch*.

As a young girl from Michigan, when I moved to New York City I was awestruck by the glamorous women I saw on the streets of Manhattan. With their beautiful hair, clothes, and jewelry, I wanted to be just like them, until I heard several of them speak one day. They had the classic high-pitched New York nasal tone that Fran Drescher took to the bank on television in *The Nanny* ("Eeow, Mistuh Sheffeeeeld ..."). The glamorous images ended right there, because voice is as much a part of the package as physical appearance. Just ask silent film matinee idol John Gilbert, who had millions of women at his feet during the 1920s (well, you can't ask him anymore because he died. But if you could ...). His annoying pinched speaking voice sounded the professional death knell of his career when "talkies" ended the silent film era. If those beautiful New York women as well as John Gilbert really cared about the complete package, they would have gone to see a vocal coach, because there's no reason that, like Eliza Doolittle in *My Fair Lady*, one's voice and diction can't improve.

Most people find nasal resonance to be irritating and prefer a voice that comes from the chest. Worried about how you sound? Put your right hand on your abdominal muscles and your left hand flat on your chest. As you speak, your left hand should feel vibrations on your chest. Say a few words. Can you feel your chest resonating? This should help to make your voice more aurally appealing.

Perhaps former presidential candidate Ross Perot should have tried this. He has a nasal, whiny voice that prevented him from ever being taken seriously by most voters ("Now, ah haeve a tax plaen fer all 'mericans …"). Al Gore was perceived by female voters as the more attractive candidate in his bid for the Presidency in 2000. But he had a tonal quality that was so flat, it dogged him for most of his 8 years as Bill Clinton's Veep as well as during his bid for the Oval Office. However, the "light went on" when he gave a tremendously energized and resonant speech at the 2004 Democratic National Convention. By the way, Hillary Clinton seems to be cranking it up the animation scale as well. Martha Stewart still needs work - as witnessed by the disastrously short run of her numbing version of the "Apprentice". She is being coached on approachability but I'm afraid the *affect* and the *effect* are still flat. History and the ratings have proven, that our favorites must look good (pleasing to the eye) and also sound good (pleasing to the ear) as well.

I was a newscaster for many years and when I was on the air, I was always asked by my talent agent to lower my pitch. They wanted that sexy, male-in-a-female body sound of a Kathleen Turner-type (sexy news, live from Detroit, Michigan

… can you imagine?). But it just wasn't me. My agent thought the lower pitch made me sound more authoritative. The audience thought it made me sound affected. It wasn't my optimum pitch, which was a few notes higher.

So, shoot for comfort and volume, and when you've achieved that and you're where you want to be, stop. Don't push, exaggerate or try to be something you're not.

Inflection/Word Stress/Variety

Meryl Streep is known as one of our greatest actors and a master of character voices. She's successfully portrayed characters with such a vast variety of accents and dialects that many people don't realize that in real life, she's not Irish, Polish, British, South African or even from Southern California - she's a Yankee from Connecticut. Her ability to seamlessly flow from one role to another appears to spring from some innate skill set. However, the truth is that she wasn't born with this skill. She learned it for her job.

I know a wonderful young lady named Avery who was born in 1991 and continues to be full of life, animation and vigor. In other words, she speaks with a fairly loud voice. She also happens to be my daughter, and I am proud to say that she has resisted switching to the "indoor voice" that society always seems to want. There is this tendency to try to blend in so that you don't vocally stand out, which makes everybody appear to be the same. If Avery loses her "outdoor voice" as she continues through her teens, she'll just have to work with a coach in her 20s to get it back. At some point we realize that to be perceived as a leader, we have to stand out, we have to be heard, and then we have to bring back everything we tried to suppress.

Most adults have learned to be polite and separate the voice from the body, as well as the mind. It's the Queen Elizabeth syndrome at play again - lost animation that needs to return to conversation and interaction in order to be memorable.

Earlier, I referred to the change in vocal animation we employ when we tell a joke. This is exactly what comedians do when they share a story or anecdote. Entertainers such as Jerry Seinfeld, Ray Romano, Jay Leno, David Letterman, Ellen DeGeneres and Kelsey Grammer (his phrasing in *Frasier* was brilliant!) are masters at vocal variety, because that's their bread and butter! Word stress and key phrasings are vital for punch lines - if they told their jokes or recited their lines in flat tones, we would never get the verbal signal that the joke was coming.

A word of caution - avoid inflection patterns. Some people end their sentences with an upward inflection (à la Reese Witherspoon in *Legally Blonde*), even when they're not asking a question. Today we call it "upspeak." In my gender seminars, I encounter it often. I ask female executives to describe the last presentation they gave and to whom. Invariably, they express frustration. They explain that they made a great point in an important meeting and no one commented or responded. They were anonymous - employing the "question mark" manner of speaking. Then a smart man in the same meeting 5 minutes later repeated the identical point, but said it with conviction. The group was impressed, and the man was ultimately promoted, while the woman withdrew and whined!

I maintain that women end their comments with question marks due to gender conditioning. We, as women, are taught to be the kinder, gentler sex - to always make it okay for somebody else to disagree with us as well as to have the last word (and then we pout when they do!). Ladies, we do it to ourselves. "Upspeak" is currently our biggest enemy to credibility, so get rid of it! Be louder, gesture more, and make your gestures mid-body - it will help direct you to diaphragmatic breathing. Sustain your volume to the end of the thought. Right now, put this book down and leave yourself a voicemail. If you hear your sentences trailing up, your credibility is heading down. Now, using volume, mid-body breathing and physical animation, leave yourself another voicemail. You should hear a difference. Practice this until you've perfected it. It's *really* important!

Some people (men more than women) attempt to sound definitive when speaking by using a downward ending, even when asking a question. The effect makes them boring and cuts off conversation. So to them I say, engage your face more! Lift your eyebrows more often and encourage yourself to smile. The body typically precedes the voice and shapes it. This new physical framing should make you sound more animated. Avoid repetitively going up and down as well. This connotes sarcasm. Know your intent when you speak so you communicate appropriately - stressing the key word or wording in a phrase.

Personalization

An integral part of word stress and inflection is personalizing your speech so it doesn't sound homogenized. A cartoon in the *New Yorker* says it best. It shows a man standing at a lectern saying, "And now I should like to depart from my prepared text and speak as a human being."

The best orators sound as if they're talking directly to you, not reading from a script. At radio stations, young DJs are instructed to speak into the microphone as if they were talking to one person - not the masses - so their show sounds more like a personal phone conversation rather than a speech. The same rule applies when you speak in front of a crowd. Legendary sportscaster Red Barber did just that when he pretended to tell his sports reports to a guy in the hallway as opposed to a large national audience. Bill Clinton does this whenever he gets in front of a group as witnessed by his ability to connect when he spoke at the 2006 funeral of Coretta Scott King.

Like many of us, I'm sure you've received those annoying telemarketing calls in the middle of dinner (when they know you're home) from poorly paid individuals who are given a script and a stack of phone numbers to cold call each evening. (What a tough way to make a living - it's like trying to sell someone insurance when their house is on fire.) You can't get a word in edgewise or have a dialogue because they have to stick to the script. This drives me (and probably you) crazy, not only because we don't want to be bothered, but who wants to sit on the phone listening to someone reciting a meaningless bunch of uninvited, disconnected words?

Yet, time and again, speakers sound just like that! Don't do it. Be conversational, just as if you're speaking to your next-door neighbor. Use short sentences and contractions. Cut *it is*, *can not* and *will not* to *it's*, *can't* and *won't*. These, in addition to frequent use of inclusive pronouns such as *we*, *us* and *our* - as opposed to exclusive pronouns *I*, *me*, and *my* - make your words sound more personal.

Don't try to make yourself look smart by including long-winded euphemisms that are hard to pronounce or understand. Which of the following would you rather listen to? "The serendipitous nature of the financial markets requires us to thoroughly investigate and avoid impulsive investment indulgences" or "The constant up and down stock market forces a potential investor to look before he leaps." Which sounds more conversational and accessible to you? Everyday English is just fine. Why trip over words, or worse, have your audience wondering what the heck you're talking about?

Jargon is the language of a specific corporate or functionary audience. But just because you're standing in front of your fellow co-workers doesn't mean you have to emulate their ongoing dysfunction by speaking in endless nonsensical language. Forget about "interface" and simply use "meeting". Avoid "internal resources" and refer to "staff". If I hear one more person use the expression "think outside the box," I'll scream. Whatever happened to "think creatively"? Kill the urge to be a member of the Dilbert crowd and join the rest of us down here on Earth, where we prefer English over corporate speak.

Minimizers of Life™

Emphatic word choices are crucial to connecting with an audience and being persuasive. Many speakers, in order to curry favor with an audience mistakenly use the converse. They substitute weak or apologetic words to introduce a thought. This can be the kiss of death! While both men and women fall into this trap, at the risk of alienating some of my female readers, I'll tell you that more often women than men put themselves into a hole by starting their declarations with phrases such as "I think", "I feel", "I might," and other such qualifiers. We like to think of ourselves as caretakers and nurturers, even while stating our opinions, so we attempt to gain favor with audience members by allowing them, even welcoming them, to disagree. As a speaker, you win no friends this way, and certainly run the risk of diminishing your impact.

Men, as well as women, constantly lessen their impact with poor word choices. For example, often you hear speeches begin with the same opening line - "I just want to tell you today about…". The speaker didn't realize it, but he/she just killed him/herself in the first 15 seconds. Nobody wants to listen to someone who minimizes his or her reason for being there.

Just or **Just a**: "Just" is a 'one-down' word that immediately says to the audience, "What I'm going to tell you is not that important." You always **must**, but you never **just**. The same goes for email and voicemail. As soon as we read or hear "just a short note," "just a quick thought," "just a reminder," the rest of the communication is diminished. Going through my email, when I see the dreaded "just a" I just delete it.

Brief or **Briefly**: "Brief" is often partnered with "just a" (i.e. "just a brief note…"). They imply you shortened something that was longer. So what are you leaving out? And if you can leave it out, why did you bother including it in the first place? You don't buy any forgiveness by telling me I'm getting the quick and easy version. Also, "brief" is a relative concept and has a different meaning for each of us. I've found that what "brief" means to a speaker can be an eternity to the audience. Don't put yourself on the clock and on the block with "brief".

Kinda: I could not believe it a short time ago when I heard a CEO say to his audience, "This is kinda important…". Either it's important or it's not. What other words could he have used? How about extremely, absolutely, hugely, decidedly. These are active words which enhance the significance of what you are about to say, as opposed to minimizing it with "kinda". And, by the way, "kinda" has a best friend - "sorta"! They are interchangeable and quite often, used together ("Well, it's kinda sorta his idea..."). Say bye-bye to both of them!

Hopefully: I can't tell you how many times I've cringed as someone has ended a presentation with something like, "Well, hopefully you now recognize the significance of this effort...". Well, I did before you told me I didn't have to! Now I'm going to revisit. Don't give your audience an out. Remember, hope is not a strategy! Jettison "hopefully" and see the difference when you say, "Now that you recognize the significance of this effort...". See how much more forceful and persuasive that is?

L'il Bit: I bet you think "l'il bit" is only used in the South! Let me tell you that I've heard it all over, and it's pervasive. "I'm just going to talk a l'il bit about...", "I'll just go into a l'il bit more detail", "I'll just l'il bit myself right out of the room!" Not only is it overly colloquial, it also immediately diminishes what comes after. Avoid it at all costs.

If you want to be effective and impactful, you should eradicate these **Minimizers of Life** from your vocabulary. Instead, use strong active words such as crucial, imperative, nexus, absolute. These words cement thoughts and support the call to action. We are not impacted by apologetic, diminishing words - while we are encouraged to act with direct, provocative modifiers.

AND Advances, BUT Reverses™

One final note on this subject. Be very careful to avoid the use of the word "but". "But" is the verbal eraser of life - it negates everything that comes before it. "That's a great thought, but…". Well, if the thought was so great, what's with "but"? Don't try to substitute "however", which is merely an extended version of "but". Try using a simple connector which has no negative connotation attached to it - *and.* "And" allows you to bridge to your thought without diminishing what was said previously. "That's a great thought, *and* we can look in additional directions on this subject…". A simple word choice changes the entire impact of the response without changing the meaning or intent.

Vocal excellence will go a long way toward making your presentations more effective and memorable. Proper breathing, appropriate vocal weight, rate, use of pauses, volume variation, expanded pitch placement, effective use of inflections and word stresses, all used in concert with each other will not only make you better understood, it will set you apart from everyone else. However, like most skills, this will not come without practice. Remember Meryl Streep - it took her many years to master her vocal inflections. You too must practice and put to use what we've discussed in this chapter. Eventually, it will become second nature. That's the goal. But you must practice, practice, practice!

CHAPTER 4

V.E.I.M. - Vocal Excellence Is Mandatory
Test Yourself!

1. How does breathing affect the sound you produce? What breathing method produces the most pleasing sound?

_____

2. Explain how weight relates to vocal animation.

_____

3. What are the dangers of speaking too slowly? Why do we prefer speakers who deliver at a rapid rate?

_____

4. Explain "dead air is good." How do pauses highlight key points?

_____

5. If your speaking voice is loud enough for everyone in the room to hear, then why change volume when you speak?

_____

6. Why is pitch so important? How can it turn off an audience?

_____

7. How does inflection and word stress affect audience comprehension?

_____

8. How can word usage turn off an audience?

_____

9. What's wrong with jargon if it makes you look smart?

_____

10. List five "Minimizers of Life? Why should they be avoided?

_____

11. Why should you avoid the use of the word "but"? What should you use instead? Why?

_____

5

Move with a Purpose!™

"Before my opponent moves, I already am moving."
Anonymous Chinese Proverb

MISSION STATEMENT
A moving target is an interesting target. Light travels faster than sound - we see it before we hear it. Effective movement can make a presentation. Ineffective or extraneous movement can kill it.

The scene is a familiar one: A packed meeting in a corporate auditorium. A screen is prominently displayed center stage. A podium with the company logo is placed downstage on the right. Entering from upstage right is Mr. Charles Chief Executive. He walks to the podium and stations himself behind it, holding onto the sides as if the podium were a life raft and he was in the middle of the ocean. He greets the audience, the lights are dimmed and the ever-present PowerPoint slide presentation begins. For the next hour, the audience is stupefied by the endless parade of data-intensive slides as described by the immobile chief executive who dares not move from behind his protective podium shield. What does the audience remember? Probably falling asleep after the 3rd or 4th slide.

Another familiar scene: Arnold Accountant has been asked to report on the quarterly results. He has prepared a copious handout along with a detailed series of visuals on an easel. In the conference room where the meeting is held, Arnold stands in front of the group, pointer in hand next to the easel, discussing each graph while swaying back and forth to some unknown and silent beat. Eventually the free hand (not holding the pointer) makes its way to his pocket where it starts drumming its own beat, independent of the swaying. He does all of this without moving from his position one centimeter! What does the audience remember? A man who clearly needed to go to the bathroom was trapped in a meeting!

What these two gentlemen seem to suffer from are two different sides of the same coin. Charles was exiled into immobility, while Arnold performed his dance of death. No movement and bad movement - both equally ineffective!

Whether you're in a large meeting, small conference, on a stage or at a table, sitting, standing or both, effective movement is a key tool to making your presentation better understood and more memorable while enhancing your executive presence. And, just as vocal excellence requires practice, effective movement is not spontaneous. It is carefully planned and rehearsed to give the impression of spontaneity while underscoring the various parts of your discussion.

One-On-One/Small Group

When conducting presentation workshops, I'm often asked how to speak more effectively when sitting at a conference table or across a desk from someone in a small meeting. Individuals in business situations seem to feel that since everyone is sitting, any overt movement is at the very least awkward and potentially unseemly. In truth, this situation is ripe for appropriate movement, which will certainly help communicate your points and make you memorable - especially when compared to the others who are too insecure or unpracticed to be physical.

In the previous chapter I discussed how to focus your key points with vocal variation. These key points can be further underscored with appropriate movement. When you're sitting around a table or across a desk, your hands become very important.

While I've talked about the reasons for gesturing in the context of body language, it's important to re-examine this important topic as it relates to communicating your message. Using hand gestures to create visual emphasis will not only make your points memorable but will make **you** memorable as well. Barack Obama, who was elected U.S. senator from Illinois in 2004, is a great image-maker. He uses his hands very effectively. Observe this the next time you have the opportunity to watch him speak. He keeps them mid-body, takes them out when he needs to make a point then returns them to their resting place. He is able to create drama, excitement and sympathy, not only with his vocal pyrotechnics but with his hands as well. When practicing your presentation, highlight the places where a physical gesture would be well positioned.

I've seen many presenters at sit-down meetings who are so highly energized that their hands become a never-ending semaphore exercise. I get the feeling they're on an aircraft carrier trying to land a small jet. This gets very distracting after a while. Just as in speaking, when you emphasize everything, nothing is emphasized. When you gesture all the time, no point is highlighted. We just remember busy hands. Find a resting place for your hands and take them out when needed. Put them back when the thought has been completed. Again, practice this!

Hand gestures aren't the only physical movements you can make at a sit-down meeting. You can still use your body even though half of it is not seen. Leaning in during a particularly important point with hands flat on the table surface coupled with a change in pitch or volume is extremely powerful. Leaning back in your chair with your arms spread is also an attention-getter. These sorts of movements can be carefully choreographed along with vocal variation. Again, you're trying to be natural in an unnatural situation. When I was a news reporter, we were taught to keep the lower part of our body relaxed while maintaining an animated upper body. During interviews, this allowed us to connect, impress and make an impact while being, essentially, stationary. Plan and practice these gestures with the appropriate timing, and you will be remembered!

Effective Movement

When you're standing in front of a group, you have a wonderful opportunity to "take the stage" as theatre people say. However, just because you're standing and they're sitting doesn't necessarily mean you will command attention. Think of how many lectures you've slept through because the speaker, although standing, was immobile and uninteresting.

As I stated earlier, a moving target is an interesting target. Our eye is immediately drawn to movement. Even when the presentation is gripping, when something else moves, we look towards it. There are few more connected experiences than going to a movie at a cinema. The screen is lit, the auditorium is dark, people are hushed (well, not always - people do seem to talk at the screen these days. I do not understand when movies became interactive, but that's for another time). The murderer is about to be caught, the verdict is about to be announced, the car is about to go over the cliff, and then someone stands up in the middle of the row to head to the bathroom! Immediately, all those who can see this are momentarily drawn to this individual's exit. It never fails - movement *always* takes focus.

Consider this when planning your presentation. Do not be afraid to "work the room." You are not required to stand in the front all the time. Move around the room. What does your audience have to do when you move? They have to follow you, and this keeps them engaged.

Movement indicates transition. When you complete a thought and are moving on to the next, a gesture - several steps in another direction, a change of focus - all communicate to the audience that you are moving on to something else. Similarly, when making a key point, a large gesture or quick movement - half turn, outstretched arms, several quick steps, energetic pointing - drives the point home. It makes you believable. You may feel it, and you may even sound like it, but if we don't see it there's a good chance that we won't buy it!

Another effective movement technique is to change levels. You can be standing in front of a group and then grab a chair and sit among them for a bit. Or, try my personal favorite: the "perch." Instead of leaning in (and thus potentially weakening your stance) to make a point, I like to sit on the corner or edge of a table. I'm still above the seated audience, but I have come closer to them and am more among them.

Just like the flailing gestures of the over-energetic seated presenter, the "dance of death" referred to earlier by our standing speaker can also be a killer. Let's face it, no matter how confident we are, a certain degree of nervousness is always felt when we get in front of a group. It's natural - and appropriate. But what do we do with this nervous energy? Well, many people merely pace back and forth. Some sway to and fro or backwards and forwards. Others put their hands in their pockets and shake their change vigorously. They have to do something! The problem is they haven't practiced appropriate movement and are just venting their energy the only way they can. You don't have to do that. You've gone over your presentation, noted when movement is called for and practiced accordingly.

Eventually, appropriate movement will become second nature and you won't have to practice it so much. But like most things, it does take effort. But these efforts pay off big dividends when effectively put to use. In theatre we call it "blocking" - purposeful and staged movement, choreographed and practiced.

Pace and Plant™

What's the lesson here? Most people think you have two choices: to either stand completely immobile, so you don't distract from your message, or run around like one of those crazed motivational speakers you see on television with the headset microphones and magnified images behind them. Fortunately, there is a happy medium: effective movement with a purpose, used strategically to maintain focus and communicate key points. I call it "Pace and Plant" - move a little, stick a lot. These movements and gestures, whether you're standing or sitting, are not spontaneous but carefully practiced to make the most of the moment.

CHAPTER 5

Move with a Purpose!
Test Yourself!

1. Why should movement be planned and not spontaneous?

    _____

2. What are three appropriate moments in a presentation when movement is necessary?

    _____

3. What should you do with your hands when not gesturing?

    _____

4. What are alternative movements you can use to make a point when at a sit-down meeting?

    _____

5. What are three ways you can 'take the stage'?

    _____

6. Explain how to coordinate appropriate movement with vocal variation.

    _____

CHAPTER 5

6

Giving Face™

"The face is the index of the mind." - Latin Saying

MISSION STATEMENT
The face is the part of you that is capable of the most effective and versatile communication. It must be used in tandem with the voice and the rest of your body. Use it well, and you'll never be forgotten. Decline to use it, and you'll be a distant memory.

To many of us accustomed to the fast-paced, highly charged and special effects-loaded movies of today's cinema, the quaint era of silent films from the early part of the 20th century seems like primitive entertainment at best. How could a bunch of people making funny faces while an organ played drippy music be considered the least bit interesting? How indeed!

How did Rudolph Valentino so excite the female (and some of the male) audience with his magnificent visage that when he died (prematurely), thousands and thousands of grieving fans wept and fainted at his funeral? How did Buster Keaton, with his perpetually woebegone expression, make audiences collapse into peals of laughter? How did Charlie Chaplin, with one look, make audiences cry and laugh at the same time?

These performers never uttered audible words in those silent films, but their facial expressions communicated volumes. Iconic film director D.W. Griffith's classic *Birth of a Nation*, which premiered in 1915, caused riots in Boston, New York and Philadelphia when it opened - and not a word was spoken.

The most effective tool we have for communication is often the most neglected. Time and time again I have seen bright, interesting and engaging people fall far short of their desired outcomes when making presentations because they neglected to, as we say, "give face." They neglected to use appropriate facial expressions to underscore vocal variation and movements when making points or transitions.

The Power of Animation

The creators of daytime dramas (soap operas) learned this lesson a long time ago. You may have wondered why the camera closes in on a character's face right before the commercial break. Some sort of cliffhanger confrontation has just taken place, some piece of crucial information has just been given up, some sort of lie has been exposed - and right before we go to commercial, the camera zooms in on the vixen, stud-muffin or villain and holds there for at least 3 seconds. During that excruciatingly long take, the character's face registers some very dramatic emotion - surprise, anger, fear, glee. This tells the audience exactly what is going on in the character's mind - all they need to know to carry them through the commercial break. There's no need for words. This piece of business was brilliantly parodied in Carol Burnett's weekly variety show, the soap opera send up, *As the Stomach Turns*. Remember those crashing organ chords as each character registered an exaggerated grimace of some sort? While it's an artificial device, it's an effective one because it leaves little doubt about what's going on with the character in a short moment, without having to write a single word of dialogue.

Remember, it's all about time. You need to be as memorable as you can be in the shortest amount of time possible. This doesn't mean you need to be excessively theatrical to get your audience's attention. However, you do need to effectively use all the tools at your disposal. We've already spoken about **vocal excellence** and **movement with a purpose**. Facial variation or "**giving face**"as we're calling it, is **the 3rd part of this triad**, and a very important one. As I mentioned earlier, light travels faster than sound - and you can *see* it before you *hear* it. When you underscore your words with appropriate facial expressions, the audience will begin to comprehend your words before you utter them. This can be a tremendous advantage, especially when you're under a time constraint.

As with gestures and movement, giving face should be practiced and prepared in advance. Your words can be given all the nuance and implicit meaning you intend with the right expression. This becomes all the more important when speaking to large groups. Actors learn to adjust their performing techniques to their venues. Performances can be very subtle and delicate in movies and television, as the camera can zoom right in to pick up the slightest movement and change in expression. In a small theatre things are kicked up a notch as the emoting has to carry over rows of seats. In a large theatre, everything has to be even bigger for the audience to appreciate what's going on. In an arena, performers have to work very hard to maintain the energy necessary to communicate to an audience of thousands. This is why a small, sweet show like *The Fantastiks* with only 6 characters would never play in a huge theatre or arena - it couldn't carry without the actors performing in an over-the-top manner, thus ruining the show. And this is why a big musical like *Phantom of the Opera* would be awful in a small theatre - it would blow out the audience.

Similarly, your presentation technique, especially in terms of facial expression, needs to be adjusted for the venue in which you're speaking. At a small sit-down meeting, you can maintain the variation but keep your expressions more tightly controlled so as not to look too histrionic (or like you're trying too hard). In a larger room or hall, your expressions need to become almost outsized to communicate effectively. I go one step further. As a woman, I wear make up (some men do too, but they need to be careful as that might send an unintended message to the audience). When I'm working with or speaking to a large group, I use more dramatic make-up to ensure that my facial expressions carry over a longer distance. It truly makes a difference. I've seen videos of myself in a big room both with lighter and more defined make-up, and more defined consistently communicates greater effectiveness. Depending on your comfort level, ladies…some blush, powder and lip gloss are mandatory. Let me debunk right now the notion that we "glow." The fact is we sweat, and there's no excuse for that.

Practice!

For those who are not trained in dramatic arts - which is most people, practicing facial expressions is awkward at best. There is a tendency to imitate the soap opera style I discussed earlier, and we feel silly. Time and time again, I've worked with individuals who were, to put it mildly, deadpan in their delivery. I've encouraged them to "kick it up a notch." During videotaping, they feel they are 'acting' when they become more animated. But once they see themselves during playback, they're amazed at how natural they look and, this is the key part, how **compelling** they've become! Spending some serious time in front of a mirror can be a great help in this area. Eyes, eyebrows, mouth, cheeks, head position - all contribute to facial expression. For example, if you want to communicate skepticism (which usually begins with "Well…."), you need to squint your eyes slightly, purse your lips and tilt your head a bit. Surprise is communicated by raised eyebrows, big eyes and a slightly opened mouth. Create a list of emotions and practice the facial expressions that go with each. Then, highlight some areas of your presentation that you feel need to carry some dramatic weight (i.e. significant sales results, a new marketing tool, greater opportunity for profits) and articulate those areas with the appropriate face - surprise, joy, excitement, etc. Then, articulate those areas without giving face. You'll see a tremendous difference!

During the most recent presidential election campaign, we were all impressed with John Kerry's oratory skills as well as the breadth of his knowledge on a myriad of topics. However, despite much coaching, his face and tone came off as somewhat impassive, resulting in an emotional disconnect. As a matter of fact, jokes were made that his face was so immobile, he made Mt. Rushmore look animated. He was saying all the right things, but they had no personal ring to them. George Bush, on the other hand, didn't have a problem with animation but hurt himself with his inappropriate facial expressions. His grimacing during the 1st debate became fodder for his critics and friends alike. After being told he had to keep his face still, during the 2nd debate the President sat with his face taut. But he had to do something to express his annoyance, so he blinked as if he just lost a contact lens. Back in 2000, Al Gore imploded with his "schoolmarmish" tut-tutting, sighing, shrugging and finger wagging. The impact of facial gesturing is enormous.

If you have a video camera, I strongly suggest that you tape yourself giving a presentation, paying special attention to your facial expressions. As you watch yourself, (no one likes to look at themselves on tape, but you'll be much more self-critical than your audience ever will) you can see for yourself when you look engaging and when you look flat. How does it feel to watch someone who looks flat as compared to someone who looks energized? The difference is quite striking.

As with movement, this takes a great deal of practice. It's not something that comes naturally to most people. However, after consistently being more expressive you won't have to practice so much, and giving face will be more automatic.

Good face can add tremendously to your executive presence.
Lack of good face can be a serious detraction.

Good face can make you memorable.
Lack of good face can make you forgettable.

Good face communicates.
Lack of good face says nothing.

CHAPTER 6

Giving Face
Test Yourself!

1. How did the silent film stars communicate so well without uttering a single word?

_____

2. Define "give face."

_____

3. If you move with energy and have a well-crafted presentation, why is "giving face" important?

_____

4. How should you adjust your facial expressions to your venue?

_____

5. How can you practice "giving face" techniques?

_____

6. Why are we more self-critical than audiences?

_____

7. When we are speaking to an audience as though they were hearing our words for the first time, what should we take into consideration?

_____

7

Controlling the Room™

"God helps those who help themselves." - Algernon Sydney

MISSION STATEMENT
*Certain things are beyond your control, but take charge of
those things you can control. Control of the venue (room set
up, technology, food service) and handling adverse situations
will enhance your effectiveness and executive presence.*

You over-schedule yourself for the day. You have a presentation to give at 3:00. You're running late and dash into the room at 2:57. The chairs are awkwardly placed giving you no space to move. There's no table for your hand-outs. There's no cable to connect your laptop to the LCD projector. All of the markers you need for the flip chart you're using are dried up. Remember the importance of the first 30 seconds we discussed at the beginning of this book? With all these adverse elements, how do you think you're going to come off? How do you think you're going to feel as you begin? Will you be able to hide your annoyance, nervousness and anxiety? Should you have to put yourself in that position?

Partnering With Your Venue™

When I give a workshop, I have a written set of requirements for my clients that include room setup and necessary equipment. Even with that, I always plan to arrive at least one-half hour early to make sure everything is in place. Despite advance notice, I usually spend the first 15 minutes moving furniture around to suit the needs of the program I am conducting that day. I make sure my technology works properly. I make sure my handouts and visual aids have an appropriate place. I check the markers to ensure that they work - and bring some extras just in case the ones I've been given don't. Then, most importantly, I walk the room to get comfortable with my surroundings.

Why do I take so much time to perform what may appear to be compulsive tasks? Simply, I need to know that the room in which I am working works for me. If something is amiss, I fix it. If something is missing, I find it - or a replacement. If something is not arranged properly, I rearrange it. I take control of the room. I call it **"partnering with your venue."**

If things are arranged so you're forced into a small corner of the room, how do you think you feel? If there is a podium set up which doesn't allow you to move freely, how do you think that affects your outreach? If the equipment you need to support your presentation is not working properly, how do you think that affects your confidence, or adds anxiety to your feelings of competence? How does it look to an audience when you have to fiddle with the PowerPoint? What do they remember about you?

Most of the time, very little in a room is nailed down. If you arrive at your presentation site and find it not to your liking, then, by all means, have things moved around to suit you. I prefer a horseshoe arrangement for audiences as it allows me close proximity to most people in the room. When size precludes this, I request chevron seating with a center aisle. This allows greater access than typical theatre style seating.

I like to have a small table at the front where I can place notes and a glass of water and "perch" (as we discussed earlier) from time to time. I also like to have two flip charts - one for my pre-made visuals and the other for those I'll be creating during the presentation.

I cite these preferences because you need to think about what you will require before you arrive. You can't show up right before a presentation and start to think about how the room might work better for you. There's not enough time. In addition, you will enhance your executive presence if you have a list of requirements that you can communicate in a timely fashion to whomever is introducing you. It will make you appear as if you've given your presentation a great deal of thought (and you have!) and are a thorough professional (and you are!).

If you arrive and see that a podium is placed too close to the edge of a platform to allow you to walk in front of it, have it moved. Don't let cables that are taped to the floor scare you. Tape is expendable - it can be ripped up and placed somewhere else. If some part of your technology doesn't work, have the individual responsible for audiovisual equipment (be sure to get that person's name before you arrive) summoned immediately to take care of the problem. If you need to have the chairs rearranged, then, by all means, have them moved (or move them yourself - I've done that quite often). In short ... make the room work for you!

Adjust to Achieve™

Now, I am aware that there are times when you don't have the luxury of making changes; the seating is fixed, the tables are stationary, etc. In such a situation, an early arrival is even more important. You must figure out how to best present, given the circumstances. You should walk around the room to see where you can move without struggling through people. You might want to do a sound check to make sure you can be heard across the room. You need to be confident that you can accomplish what you need to, given the circumstances. Never let your audience see you sweat, because if you do, that's all they'll remember. They won't miss anything they don't see, so if things aren't exactly the way you would like, don't bring it to their attention - it will only serve to diminish you and make your audience uncomfortable. Adjust to achieve - always have a backup plan - and remember to be flexible! Try not to think in a linear fashion, rather, think how you can accomplish your desired outcome, given the circumstances. No matter how hard you try or how detailed your pre-presentation requirements, things sometimes go awry. But that's okay, because you have a methodology to get around these issues and still accomplish your goal effectively.

I will never forget the time I was scheduled to run a workshop as part of a three day conference. My presentation was the last part of the program, after which the attendees would depart for the various transportation terminals that would carry them home. Even though I always request not being scheduled at the end of a conference, this isn't always honored. At any rate, per usual I checked the room and rearranged things as best I could. I went to get some coffee, and before I returned to the room the client stopped me in the hall. He informed me that I should plan to start one half hour later and end one half hour earlier. Evidently they had some things they needed to get done before I began, and had to depart early in order to make connections. So I had to cut an entire hour from a 3 hour presentation - at the last minute, I might add! I took a deep breath and said okay. 30 minutes later, I returned to the room to find that everyone's luggage was blocking the aisles and that moving throughout the room would be impossible. To make matters worse, the individual speaking before me announced that box lunches were available on a table in the hall, that they needed to be checked out by 11:30 and then she thanked them for attending - effectively ending the conference!! She closed with, "We'll take a little break and then have some fun with Tamara!" I was furious, but what could I do?

I would say that 50% of the attendees vanished (after practically being told they could go), leaving me in a luggage-filled room with half of the group. So… remembering my desired outcome, I quickly improvised. I had those who decided to stay come forward and sit up front. I got out my flip chart and asked them what their concerns were and what they had questions about and proceeded to conduct a truncated version of my planned workshop, directly addressing their issues. And it proved to be a smashing success. The attendees felt they got what they needed and I looked like I knew what I was doing.

I can be relaxed about it now. But at the time, I was seething. Not only had my time been cut by a third, but the room was made non-navigable. Perhaps most distressing, I was turned into an optional afterthought by the individual who spoke before me. I was totally diminished. However, my feelings were not the primary issue at the time. Remember, my desired outcome was an effective presentation workshop for the attendees. So I thrust aside my rage and worked the room the best I could. Mission accomplished! However, if I had carried my anger and frustration into the workshop, it would've been an uncomfortable waste of time for everyone.

Be aware of trends, and if they don't work for you, don't subscribe to them. Case in point: it is currently very popular to have audiences at large meetings seated at round tables of 8-10 people. The effect is a cavernous cabaret which forces the speaker into the role of night club entertainer, dancing and weaving among the participants. This format encourages interaction, but unfortunately, not with the speaker. These small pods tend to get very intimate with each other and ignore the presenter. Based on experience, advocate for horseshoe seating for smaller settings or a chevron arrangement with a center aisle for groups over 25.

The moral here is simply that you need to take control of your surroundings as much as possible. You need to make them work for you. If you can't, you need to adjust to achieve and not let adverse circumstances get in the way of your effectiveness. Remember, your feelings of being slighted, thwarted, diminished or otherwise are not the issue - save them for later.

When food is part of the program, special care needs to be taken. Psychologist Abraham Maslow created the human "hierarchy of needs," and being fed ranks right at the top of that list. When it's mealtime, people are thinking about food and not about what you have to say. Work with the caterer, restaurant or food service provider to plan the meal. Make sure your audience has time to eat something before you speak - a salad or small 1st course. If possible, arrange for food that is relatively simple to eat so that people are concentrating less on eating and more on you. At dinner meetings, limit the cocktail hour so your audience will be less likely to suffer the effects of drinking. Most importantly, manage your expectations. Don't plan an overly ambitious agenda. If you do, then you and your audience will walk away full, but not satisfied.

Recognize the "Elephant in the Room"

Quite simply - stuff happens. Audience members arrive late and leave early, projector bulbs blow out, things drop on the floor, cellphones and pagers make loud noises, and so on. These are the sorts of things that can drive a presenter crazy...and if they do, you'd better find another line of work because all the audience will remember is that you got rattled when something happened.

Whenever a door opens or someone enters a room, where do everyone's eyes go? Right to the door! It never fails. So, instead of having this interruption throw you and make you uncomfortable, acknowledge the newcomer with a friendly smile, point out an empty seat and let him or her know what you are discussing. This accomplishes two things at once, it allows you to repeat a key point that might bear repeating and it also brings the audience member up to date so he or she doesn't have to ask a neighbor, further disturbing the presentation. If a cellphone goes off, don't raise your voice to cover the sound and pretend that nobody heard it. Simply smile and say that you know that keeping in constant touch is a cost of doing business these days, but that you need to ask everyone to either turn their phones off or, if absolutely necessary, put them on vibrate. If they must take the call, ask them to sit as close to a door as possible so they can make a quick exit to carry on a conversation. If you're giving your presentation in one of those large rooms with sliding walls, and there is a loud meeting being conducted on the other side of one of your walls, don't simply scream over the noise. Stop your meeting for a moment, ask the people on the other side of the wall if they could move the loudspeakers or the TV monitor or even just keep it down a little. I'm sure they'd appreciate it if you did the same. Let your audience know that you're trying to do something about the competing distractions. Boy will they love you for that!

I was attending a fund-raiser for my husband's Ivy League university recently, and a major donor, who was also the CEO of his own company, was speaking.

He was using some wireless amplification equipment, and in the middle of his presentation we heard this series of loud pops, like gunshots, through the speakers. Without missing a beat, the speaker said, "I don't know whether to duck or continue...I wasn't aware my earnings were that disappointing." The crowd loved it and he had them eating out of his hand.

Last year I was called in to consult on a major product launch. I was to coach the senior executives on their presentations to the rank and file. These presentations are important because they encourage the sales force and account executives to go all out marketing and promoting the product. For those who are unfamiliar with the format of these events, let me say that they are generally major theatrical presentations complete with singers and dancers as well as elaborate sets. The CEO of the company was in the middle of his cheerleading effort when the entire set behind him became unhitched and crashed to the stage. A lesser man would have exited very quickly. He merely faced his audience and said, "Either we're having an earthquake (the event was in California) or they're trying to tell me something. I know I've always had a few screws loose, but that shouldn't apply to the stage set as well!" The audience roared and the meeting was deemed a tremendous success.

Pretend a mishap or disturbing occurrence didn't happen, and all the audience will think about is *that* occurrence. Acknowledging the situation, and showing the audience that it didn't bother you will give them permission to move on and not focus on whatever the mishap was. Quite simply, acknowledge the "elephant in the room." I'll never forget the streaker at the Academy Awards some years ago. The urbane and witty British actor, David Niven was in the middle of a presentation when a naked man ran across the stage behind him.

Mr. Niven merely raised his eyebrows, looked at the audience and said, "Well, here's a first - the naked truth at the Oscars." It was a glorious moment.

Not long ago, the *Today Show* had a weekend feature called "Caring for Your Pets." Warren, the pet expert, came on to discuss issues around families and new pets. To that end, he brought a whole bunch of energetic puppies onto the set. While Warren and the weekend anchor were talking, one of the puppies started circling at the corner of the mat where the dogs were playing and conspicuously relieved himself, leaving a steaming pile behind. The anchor saw this and tried to acknowledge it, but Warren didn't want his presentation to be interrupted, so he pretended it hadn't happened. The other dogs started sniffing around the pile and soon got their paws in it. To make matters worse, they began jumping on the anchorman, covering his expensive suit with puppy poop, which the camera picked up. All Warren could say was that he was trying very hard not to look over there and kept going. Well, you know what the audience was looking at - do you think they heard a word Warren was saying? The anchor clearly had some of the mess from the puppies on his hands and his pants, but Warren didn't care - he just needed to get through his talk! As you can imagine, the segment was a disaster. You might say it went to the dogs or - pardon the pun - ended up in the toilet!

What should they have done? Warren could have incorporated the situation into his talk and said something about puppy training and accidents or asked one of the stagehands to sweep away the mess. The distraction would've been minimized and the show could've continued as planned. Linear thinking made this impossible, and the result was not the desired outcome. So, when manure happens - and it will in some form or another, acknowledge it, get rid of it, and move on!

Controlling the Room
Test Yourself!

1. Why is it important to communicate your presentation needs in advance of your presentation?

   _____

2. When you arrive at your presentation site, what do you need to accomplish before your presentation begins?

   _____

3. What do you do if you're not able to arrange the room to your satisfaction?

   _____

4. What is meant by "adjust to achieve"?

   _____

5. How can the desired outcome be obscured by a personal agenda?

   _____

6. How can you best control food service during a presentation?

   _____

7. What is meant by the "elephant in the room"?

_____

8. What is the best way to handle distractions?

_____

8

YOU Are the Star, Not the Visuals™

"We are drowning in information, but starved for knowledge."
John Naisbitt

MISSION STATEMENT
A good presenter is not upstaged by his/her visuals. No one
will compliment you on your slides; however, inappropriate
use of visuals can relegate you to obscurity.

I am "of an age," that when I was in elementary school, technology was quite primitive relative to today's bells and whistles. Back then I loved it when the teacher brought out the projector to show us movies or the ubiquitous film strips. It meant I could doodle, daydream, write a silly poem about a boy I had a crush on, or even, dare I say, take a quick nap. The privacy created by the darkened room gave me license to do so many things that were not available to me during a regular class.

Effective Use of Visual Aids

As adults, we are somewhat more restrained during meetings with visuals. But when your audience walks into a meeting room and sees a screen with the PowerPoint opening slide already displayed, you can bet that they'll be thinking about how many emails they'll be able to send on their Blackberries or how they can discretely complete their agenda during your slideshow for another meeting they'll be conducting later.

I will never forget participating in a conference not too long ago when, once again, I was last on the program (are they trying to tell me something?). Prior to my workshop with a group of doctors, a distinguished physician was discussing the effects of the nicotine patch on pregnant women. His goal was to convince the physicians that there was no danger associated with this product's use during pregnancy. I decided to listen to this speaker so I could perhaps reference 1 or 2 of his points during my presentation and establish a quick connection. This very learned, intelligent speaker spent *2 hours* going through slides in a darkened room. The lights were never on and the projector was never off during the entire time this man spoke. It was the most ossifying experience of my professional life. Occasionally, some brave soul asked a question, but the speaker went on and on and on, slide after slide after slide. When the lights were finally turned back on, the entire audience opened their eyes, blinked and stretched as if they had been hanging out with Rip Van Winkle, asleep for the past 20 years! What do you think those poor doctors remembered from that presentation?

Let's face it. We have become PowerPoint dependent (as I like to say, too much Power and too little Point!). Every corporation in every area of its operations has a 'deck' of slides for some presentation. This all-important deck has become the cornerstone of most every corporate meeting, and when you walk into a room with that LCD projector humming, honestly, the first thing you think is, "Here we go again ...". Is that memorable in the least?

Now, I'm not going on a crusade against slide presentations. Studies have shown that when you see something, you have a 40% greater chance of remembering it than if you just hear it. The visual impact of good slides during a well-presented meeting can be enormous. What I am crusading against is the over-use of this "PowerPoint parade" as a crutch for poor speakers. Again and again, I've seen valuable information during a presentation go completely unheard because the speaker stood at a podium for an hour in a dark room with the ever-present laser pointer and ran a slideshow. There was no interaction with the audience. There were too many slides for the audience to take in. The slides had complete sentences on them and were therefore read by the speaker. It would have been simpler if the speaker had merely given out hard copies of his slides to the audience and said, "Take these and go over them. Call me with any questions. Thank you." That would've saved everyone a great deal of time.

I will share with you several guidelines that will help to distinguish you from your slides - tips that will have the audience walk away remembering you and your key points, as opposed to what animation tricks you used on the 2nd quarter sales results slides ("I really liked the exploding profit figures, but the bouncing loss numbers were a bit much.").

The projector should be off at the beginning and end of the meeting. The presentation should commence and conclude with you, not a slide. When a slide is on the screen, even if it's a title slide (name of presenter, company, date, subject - why do they bother with those, it's all information we already know!), people are looking at the screen and not you. It's very hard to compete with a slide, so start with a blank screen for the focus to be on you. If you are in a very large venue, say north of 150 attendees, then you may use a slide as your backdrop - just keep it as simple as possible. View it as a curtain that will come up when the real show starts.

A podium is a great home base, but you need not spend the entire presentation behind it. Always start in front of the podium. If you're just using a laptop on a table, start in front of that. Remember the first 30 seconds. It's important for you to make the connection with the audience, and that connection will be thwarted if you can't be seen.

Laser Pointer Dependency™

Once you start using the slides, guide the audience with your commentary, not with your laser pointer. Let me say here that there should be no complete sentences on your slides, merely fragments to pique your commentary. You are the interpreter; you are the expert.

Speaking of laser pointers, there is nothing I find more annoying. We can't hold them still, the red dot shakes all over the screen, as we try to find the target. Worse yet, we forget we have the button depressed and end up blinding the entire first row. It's overused, it gives the audience a headache and it sucks the animation out of the speaker. If you must use it, pick it up when you need it, put it down when you don't. If you get a really busy slide that absolutely requires the use of a pointer, quickly point to the area where you want the audience to focus, reference the information and release the pointer. But truly, if a slide is that busy, your first instinct should be to edit it down or perhaps break it apart into several slides. A laser pointer **never** makes a bad slide better.

Both hands free is most effective, and you'll find, in the majority of cases that your hand and body can guide the audience much more effectively than the laser pointer. This approach puts you back in control, and allows your voice to be more animated.

Slide Management

While good slides are great to use, we often have too much of a good thing when we use too many slides. I recently returned from conducting a presentation skills workshop with an amazingly intelligent, and I might add, intimidating group of medical professionals. However, smart does not equate to engaging. The presenters used vast amounts of text on their slides - to a numbing effect. Coupled with the shaky red dot emanating from the ubiquitous laser pointer, the presenters began to antagonize each other. The conference soon deteriorated into a cerebral joust. I think they were interrupting each other just to stay awake. Afterwards, one of the "thought leaders" asked me what happened and how to make it better going forward. I referred him to a pivotal study that shows that the **optimum number of slides** you should use during a presentation, on average, is **1 every 3 minutes**. The brain absorbs the information best at that rate of slide exposure. I realize that this is sometimes difficult to manage. However, no matter how much information you wish to communicate during a particular presentation, you dare not use more than 1 slide per minute, 1 every 2 is better, 1 every 3 is best. I'm not saying that discussion is limited to a steady 1 minute per slide; that's just not possible with most presentations. We expect you will expand and contract. The rule of thumb is based on the *total* number of slides divided by the *total* number of minutes you're speaking. The brain can't take in any more than that, and your message will be obscured. Less is more, less is more, less is more! Don't make your agenda too ambitious or you'll end up wasting everyone's time. If you don't intend to show a slide for at least 30 seconds, delete it from your deck. All people will remember is that you tried to cram too much into the time you had, and they'll resent it. Is that the memory you'd like to leave with your audience?

Every time I give this next little trick, members of my workshops tell me that it, alone, was worth the entire day. Remember when we discussed earlier that as long as a slide is being displayed on the screen, the audience is looking at the slide and not you? You could be dancing the Macarena with Secretary of State Condi Rice and they'd still be looking at the slide. So, if you find that your presentation starts veering off into a discussion that doesn't reference the slide for 30 seconds or more, then press the 'B' (for blank) key on your laptop, and the slide will disappear. Press the 'B' key again and the slide will magically reappear. You'll be amazed how the heads will twist in your direction as soon as you blank the slide and how they'll twist back just as quickly when the slide returns. Also, don't be afraid to raise the lights a bit if the discussion continues. The lights eliminate the anonymity and return the focus to you.

Here's another technology trick. More often than not, a speaker during a slide presentation traps him or herself in a box between the screen and computer. During the entire talk, they perform what I call the death march between the corner of the screen and the laptop. Back and forth, back and forth - that's all they do. The whole focus centers on getting back to the laptop in time to change the next slide. It's redundant, predictable, boring and unmemorable. (I call it the 'vector of death'.) To get around this, I suggest you purchase one of those wireless remote slide changers ("clickers"). They are available at any store that sells computers and accessories and are relatively inexpensive. Armed with this device, you can advance or go back to a slide at any point in the room. They are also equipped with another button which will allow you to 'blank' the slide when you choose - much like the 'B' key on the computer. You can move around, keeping people focused on you, and you become more focused on the message - no longer sprinting to the laptop to change the slides. You will appear more in control, and once again, your executive presence is enhanced. The trick here is not to overuse your new toy. Don't cram in more slides because it's so much fun to be able to "magically" advance them, and be sure to put it down when making key points. Remember, unencumbered hands are your best visual aids! Depending on the size of the meeting, end your presentation with a logo slide or no slide at all. In a smaller venue, after your final slide, press 'B' on your computer to blank the slide or turn off the projector - the hum of those things is very distracting. You should then take "center stage" and deliver your planned close, out from behind the podium, or in front of the table with the laptop. Once again, the meeting begins with you and ends with you, not the slide. I've even seen slides that say "Thank you" - wouldn't it be more personal and memorable if you just *said* it, and *meant* it? Referring back to my primacy/recency discussion in Chapter 1, *you* are what the audience will remember most, not a muddle of slides. Think about it: Would Martin Luther King, Jr., have had the same impact if he had uttered, "I have a dream…next slide…"?

Depending on your desired outcome, good slides shown in moderation with energy and audience interaction can be extremely beneficial. Bad slides shown in excess with the death march can be lethal - literally! Take the case of a NASA PowerPoint presentation, as discussed in a recent New York Times article titled, "The Level of Discourse Continues to Slide." The article maintains that cluttered slides spelled disaster for the space shuttle Columbia. A crucial piece of information regarding the huge size of the chunk of foam that had broken off from the heat shield was "relegated to the last point on the slide, squeezed into insignificance." An independent board investigating the Columbia disaster later wrote, "It is easy to understand how a senior manager might have read this PowerPoint slide and not have realized that it addressed a life-threatening situation."

Confidence in your information and careful preparation can help you weed out unnecessary slides, calling attention to the more important ones. Remember, the audience doesn't miss something if they don't see it. Think carefully about which slides are really important, and use only those. The result could be more lasting and important than you imagined!

A final note on slides - I'm sure you've been to meetings when something has gone wrong with the technology and you've had to sit through what seemed to be an endless delay, while the speaker fiddled with his or her computer. Audiences have very little tolerance for technical glitches or meltdowns. They make the audience nervous and the speaker look foolish. If you find your technology is not working, do not spend too much time trying to fix it. Always have a hard copy of your slides at the ready and be prepared to continue your presentation with the copy as a guide. Your audience will be impressed with your flexibility, and without the slides you will have the opportunity to connect more solidly.

When using a flip chart, after you have finished referencing a particular page, flip it over the top, out of view. I have been to so many meetings where they post pithy flip chart pages around the room as motivational tools or more often to show how "busy" they've been. This can be very distracting. If you use hand-held visual aids for small group meetings or one-on-one conferences, be sure to guide your audience with your hand by pointing where you want their eyes to go, then place the aid face down when you're finished. Just like the PowerPoint slides, when a visual aid is visible, that is what your audience will focus on, not you. Control the flow by controlling the visual aid.

Here's a quick word on handouts. I strongly urge you not to distribute handouts until the end of your presentation. If you distribute any sort of handout and ask the audience to "follow along," all they are going to do is read ahead and make a lot of paper rustling noise while they're doing it. Once they finish they will put the handout down and not listen to you because they now "know it all." In essence, you've allowed them to "self study." And once they leave, guess what they do with the handout? It gets left behind. Make sure you are given a table on which you can place your handouts, and encourage the audience to take them as they depart. You can't control whether or not they'll read them, but you can be sure they won't disrupt your presentation. If the group insists on handouts, distribute them in "incremental chunks." This will help them stay with you, and importantly, not allow them to skip to the end.

Visual aids should be just that - aids. If you hide behind your technology, you will be anonymous. But effective use of good slides and visuals will positively enhance your desired outcome and help communicate your key points.

YOU Are the Star, Not the Visuals
Test Yourself!

1. How does a darkened room affect your audience?

_____

2. Why are most slide presentations not memorable?

_____

3. How do you blank a slide during a presentation?

_____

4. How can you interact with the audience during a slide presentation?

_____

5. How do you start and end your presentation when using slides?

_____

6. What is the optimum number of slides you should use during a presentation?

_____

7. How can a speaker become more "mobile" during a slide presentation? Why is that important?

   _____

8. Why should flip chart pages and hand-held visuals be removed after discussion of them has ceased?

   _____

9. Why should you avoid distributing handouts during a meeting?

   _____

9

Advanced Facilitation
"Influence Without Authority"

"Facilitation is a secret exercise of power..."
C. Wright Mills

MISSION STATEMENT
*Once you have your presentation down pat, you can then concentrate
on 'working the room' - facilitating the meeting so you can reach
your desired outcome with as many participants as possible.*

Y ou've practiced and practiced. You've worked on "rehearsed spontaneity", "organize for impact," "passion for your subject" and "vocal variation." Your personal packaging is impeccable. Your message is compelling with a "mission in mind" and a "benefit to the audience." Your visuals are at the ready to support your key points. But, are you ready? Well, at least you're ready to begin. However, the subtlest and most complex part of your job is ahead of you - the ability to "read the room" - that is, the continual assessment of your audience as your presentation unfolds. Are they engaged? Have you lost some to other tasks or sidebar conversations? Are you reaching the key decision-makers? Do they understand and believe you? Are you perceiving and dealing with push-back? Are you picking up the 'active listening' signals? Successful facilitation of your audience - be it one or many - will determine whether or not you will achieve your desired outcome.

The key to facilitation is the ability to convey confidence, persuasiveness and manage the participants to achieve your desired outcome without having the final say - as opposed to the last word. We call this **"influencing without authority"**.

At the risk of beating a dead horse - but then again, one of our major mantras is "repetition builds retention" - you cannot effectively facilitate if you're shaky on your presentation. If you're busy thinking about what comes next, you cannot be thinking about what's going on in the room. If you have to keep looking at your slides, then you can't be focused on your audience. Successful facilitation is based on a foundation of successful preparation. So, … if you're ready for prime time, then you're ready to facilitate.

Be a Good Room-M.A.T.E.™

Our approach to facilitation is based on a concept we have branded, called "Room-**M.A.T.E.S.**" - **M**oving **A**head w/**T**imely and **E**volved **S**kills™. As a presenter, you need to be a good "Room-MATE" in order to successfully connect with an audience.

Have you earned *the right to be in the room?* Namely, does your personal equity qualify you to be in front of your audience? Does your audience understand the benefit to them by listening to you? Will your words resonate, as a result? If you're speaking to an audience as someone from the 'outside', equity can be established by having an 'insider' introduce you. Remember the old saying, "god helps those who help themselves" - make sure you have a short prepared introduction ready which will enhance your credibility and make it simple for the introducer. The intro should be immediately followed by you, stating the benefits the audience will receive by listening/participating.

If you're speaking to an audience as an 'insider', it's helpful if your audience knows, in advance, what you're talking about and why you're talking about it. A simple email can accomplish this - announcing your presentation and framing it - before you utter a word.

The second aspect of "Room-MATES" is that there should be *no 'wrong' in the room*. Audience members should feel free to participate without being criticized, minimized or made to feel ignorant. A risk-free environment encourages engagement and will further connect you to your audience.

When the subject matter or subsequent discussion might potentially bring up sensitive or confidential information, it's very important to clarify *the sanctity of the room*. To paraphrase the Las Vegas tourism mantra, *"what's said in the room stays in the room"*. Your audience will certainly be less liable to engage with you if they feel that their comments might be repeated or shared with anyone outside.

Finally, it's important to level set the expectations by *creating the walls of the room*. In your role, you can establish a desired outcome as part of your partnership with the audience. But the boundaries must be set. If you make promises on unrealistic deliverables, you seriously risk your credibility and equity. Only promise what you can reasonably deliver and no more.

By adhering to the Room-M.A.T.E.S's concepts, you will be a more welcome presence as an insider or outsider and will enhance your engagement. You will be welcome, credible and perceived as value added, even before you get into the 'meat' of your presentation.

Social Facilitation

We've already discussed the importance of time earlier in this book. Time is a commodity of which we cannot get enough. As a result, we have a tendency to multi-task at every given opportunity. It's extremely difficult to engage your entire audience if you have some multitaskers doing other things from the get-go. You will mostly find them towards the back of the room. Why do people choose to sit in the back? They have plans! They have their laptops, blackberries, cellphones, reports, at the ready. If they don't like what they hear in the first 30 to 60 seconds, they have back-up. And since they have the least proximity to the speaker, they feel they have a cloak of anonymity and they won't hesitate to use it!

The strategy here is to work the room from the back to the front. Think about it. When was the last time you sat in the front - or next to the key speaker/decision-maker - at a meeting? Probably when you were really interested in the meeting, when you planned on being engaged, when you had something you wished to contribute. The 'front-sitters' need the least amount of engagement facilitation because they're the most apt to be attentive. By starting in the rear (or furthest away from the speaker) with vectoring eye contact, gestures, voice projection and movement, you have a greater likelihood of engaging those least apt to be attentive. There's even a term for this: "social facilitation."

It's important to engage the entire audience before you begin any slide presentation. The lowered lights provide an additional cloak of anonymity and therefore, you have to be more animated to compete with the slide. As we discussed in an earlier chapter on visuals, appropriate movement will help elevate your status and avoid "speaker shrinkage." During your presentation, you need to constantly check in with the back of the room to ensure you haven't lost them along the way.

Recently, I was working with a group of doctors who were being considered as potential key opinion leaders by a large pharmaceutical firm. During the portion of my session on slide facilitation, I worked my way to the back of the room and immediately noticed folders being shut and participants straightening up in their seats. After the program, one of the physicians remarked that this was the first time they had ever had a speaker who was using PowerPoint, move away from the screen and actually walk towards the rear of the room. When I asked her why she felt this was significant, she told me that my proximity forced her to sit up and pay greater attention, and she intended to do this whenever she spoke.

Everyone Loves a Good Story

Whether or not you use visuals, there are several other ways to connect with an audience from the outset. For example, you could cite a startling statistic: "Did you know that divorced men are 10 times as likely to remarry as divorced women?", use an open probe: "How many of you are responsible for children from another marriage?", or tell a story - a compelling narrative that exemplifies the main point of your presentation, a story with a moral to the audience. All of these encourage the participants to be interactive up front, but also makes you and your message more credible.

Here's an example of an actual story used to connect with an audience. Several years ago, I consulted for a large corporation setting up health clinics in inner-city schools. These clinics would provide needed healthcare services to urban young people. Now, if you're running a health clinic in a high school where there are sexually active teenagers, the distribution of condoms would certainly become part of the services offered. Well, the press got wind of this and all they could talk about was that the XYZ Company was promoting teenage sex by handing out condoms. The company spokesperson was due to give a press conference on a variety of initiatives they sponsored in California and was scared to death that the entire session would be focused on the condom issue. She asked me to help diffuse the situation. I counseled her to tell a provocative and compelling story at the very beginning of the conference which proved to be extremely effective.

Of course, the first reporter to ask a question brought up the condom issue. But my trainee was ready. She said, "You know, while the condom distribution program is worthy of discussion, what is equally worthy of discussion is an 8 year old boy named Juan. In our clinics, we see children from grades K through 12. Juan lives in South Central L.A. and last week he came into one of our clinics complaining of sudden hearing loss. His right ear was checked and nothing unusual was found. However, when the nurse examined his left ear, she found a decaying cockroach which had imbedded itself deep in his ear canal. Once removed, he was given the appropriate antibiotics and his hearing returned to normal. Clearly, when the rats weren't biting him, the roaches were. Now, if you want to talk about condoms, go ahead!" Of course, no one did. My client had diffused the situation and her audience was riveted. Take a lesson from this and facilitate your audience by engaging up-front.

Look For Signals

As you go through your presentation, it's important to check out the body language of the audience, especially key decision-makers. Are they nodding and/or taking notes? Are they looking at their watches and/or yawning? Are they crossing and uncrossing their legs with great frequency? You need to pay attention to these cues. You may need to take an unscheduled break - they may be crossing their legs because they have to use the bathroom or they may be yawning because it's their 5th meeting of the day and need a break.

In the chapter titled "Move With a Purpose," we discussed the importance of strategically placed movement. If you see part of your audience drifting away, a step in their direction will help bring them back - just like proximity which increases attention during a slide presentation! Comments directed towards the area of "disengagement" will help to shepherd the lost sheep back to you. Additional animation and vocal variation will kick things up a notch. Remember, an audience does not walk into a presentation in a deceased state. It is the speaker who kills them. It is up to you to revive them as well.

Periodically, ask simple probing questions to ensure that people are listening. When answers are given, praise and paraphrase them! Remember, there is no wrong in the room. When people are praised, they become your friend and will remain engaged.

Manage Push-back

During my workshops, I occasionally get push-back from participants who feel they "know better." More often than not, these individuals are looking for attention and recognition, or wish to let me know what it's like in "their world". In these situations, I am always careful to let them know that there's more than one way to "skin a cat". And that we're basically saying the same thing, although the timing may be slightly different, or the emphasis may vary. I go out of my way to praise their initiative and say that if it works for them - keep on doing it. What we discuss during these sessions is not behavior modification, but awareness. The awareness can be tailored to their style and situation. 99 times out of 100 this leaves them beaming and enhances my credibility. Give participants credit for contributing, even if it appears they're contradicting you. Strategically bring it back to your point, while allowing it to coexist with their point of view. You will have given up nothing and gained an ally.

Effective Listening

There are times when the presentation goes off on what may be perceived as a tangent. Often, these tangents are productive. Sometimes, however, they are the product of a participant with an agenda and/or ego. A key facilitation strategy is to learn how to transition the presentation back to you. President Bush has learned how to do this well. For example, when introducing him, a speaker might say, "Ladies and Gentlemen, the sunny state of Florida welcomes President George W. Bush!" After the applause, the President might predictably say, "It certainly is 'sunny' today, just the way 'sunny' is how every child should feel when they're on their way to school…no child should be left behind." Newscasters are superb at transitions. You might hear a story about a rockslide in northern California. The anchor will then quickly follow up by saying, "And the defendants in the Smith trial had a rocky day as well…" and go on to discuss that story. Pick out a key word in the tangent which can bring the discussion back to you and back on track. We call this *bridging and redirecting*.

Say you're at a PTA meeting leading a discussion on the need for a more intensive world cultures curriculum. A member of the audience raises his hand and says, "I don't understand why we're stressing world cultures when most of our kids can't name the capitals of all 50 states. That's the problem today. We're so busy trying to understand the customs of other countries, we don't take time to develop our kids' loyalty to the US. Let's put our culture first, I say!" An effective way to bridge and redirect might be to say, "And the only way our culture can be first is if we have a clear awareness of the culture of others. We cannot live in a cultural vacuum and function in the world today." The bridging phrase was "our culture first," and it was used to redirect the conversation back to the need for greater cultural understanding. In order to successfully bridge and redirect you must listen attentively. If you don't, you won't be able to pick out the bridge word which will allow you to redirect. You need to be as attentive to your audience as you wish them to be to you. Effective listening is mandatory for successful bridging and redirecting. Your audience will appreciate it, as well.

You will gain tremendous credibility with an audience if you can show them that you're listening to them. Another way to do this is by a process we call "looping." By looping back to a comment or question made earlier by an audience member, it demonstrates that you remember what someone has said, and you're able to validate it by using it in your remarks. At this same PTA meeting, suppose another audience member (John) says, "Since the financial markets now run 24/7, it makes sense to understand what goes on around the world so we can do business in a global marketplace. Our kids should understand this." Much later on in the discussion, the subject of world music comes up. You might then be able to loop back to the earlier comment by saying, "In many countries, music and other art forms are government supported, but unfortunately in this country, public funds are not always available. So, John's comment on the need for familiarity with the world financial markets could also introduce the notion of corporate/

private support of arts endeavors." John feels like a hero and you get credit for listening and looping.

Above all, most people feel the need to be heard. You can let someone know you hear them without necessarily praising their point. Non-judgmental terms such as **valid**, **interesting**, and **fair** will tell the participant that their comments were recognized without the ubiquitous "Great point!" - which really wasn't great at all - followed by the dreaded, "but…". This leaves the participant wondering, "If my point was so great, what's with the 'but'?". A skilled facilitator will make the participants feel heard without necessarily giving value to points which detract from the presenter's message. However, a skilled facilitator will achieve greater credibility and equity by drawing upon the individual and/or collective knowledge base of participants who support the message. He/she makes it appear that the points made are the group's ideas. You can't create better buy-in than that!

Dialogue Not Monologue™

Your ability to achieve your desired outcome, while largely dependent on preparation, is also determined by how well you facilitate. "Influencing Without Authority" is a product of being a good "Room-MATE," being skilled at reading a room and ensuring that participants are engaged and actively listening. Presentation is dialogue, not monologue, and the only way to have a dialogue end up in your favor is to manage its outcome with buy-in from the participants. This doesn't always happen because your points are well-taken. It happens when you've facilitated these well-taken points in such a way that your audience's needs are factored into your response. Don't forget - it's not about you - it's always about them!

CHAPTER 9

Advanced Facilitation
Test Yourself!

1. Why does facilitation depend on good preparation?

   _____

2. What are the four concepts of "Room-**M.A.T.E.S**?"

   _____

3. Why is it important to reassure an audience that what's said in the **room**, stays in the **room**?

   _____

4. Why is it important to engage the participants in the rear of the room and work forward?

   _____

5. Discuss the three ways to immediately engage an audience.

   _____

6. How can effective movement re-engage members of the audience?

   _____

7. How can you facilitate push-back to work in your favor?

_____

8. Give an example of bridging and redirecting.

_____

9. What is the danger in over-praising a point that is not worthy of praise? How can you avoid this?

_____

10. What is a result of drawing upon the collective knowledge base of the audience?

_____

10

Enlist to Lead™
"Elevate the Status of the Group"

"Never let the other fellow set the agenda."
James Baker

MISSION STATEMENT
Dynamic group involvement skills ensures focus,
consensus and commitment to action.

Now that you have elevated your status as an effective branded presenter, you need to ensure that when you conduct a meeting, you elevate the status of the group as well. Meetings are tricky - we all hate them - yet we attend them almost every day. The complaint I hear about meetings most often is that they're a waste of time and nothing gets accomplished. This is generally because whoever is leading the meeting hasn't a clue about how to engage a group properly. A skilled meeting leader must understand:

+ How to keep participants excited about participating in the process
+ How to keep participants focused and involved
+ How to phrase and ask questions that challenge without intimidating
+ How to guide and not overpower
+ How to manage and resolve conflict
+ How to deal with "drop-outs" and disrupters
+ How to ensure commitment to action

These are fundamental skills which help participants in any meeting achieve maximum results against any agenda set by you. By mastering them, your meetings will become time-efficient, productive, engaging and will assure the commitment of each and every participant.

The following is a set of 12 concepts that constitute a comprehensive methodology you can apply before or during any meeting or conference. Please use these concepts to achieve positive results with groups.

Preparation Equals Relaxation™

You should always go into a meeting with a clear mission in mind - one that indicates a benefit to the audience. The benefit should be stated up front with the entire meeting steered toward accomplishing the mission. All technology (PowerPoint, videos, etc.) should be tested on-site in advance. In addition to complete familiarity of meeting subject matter, you need to have complete familiarity with the personal style of the individual participants in order to maximize output, and anticipate roadblocks and competing agendas. You, as the team leader, must have highly developed presentation skills in order to keep the meeting engaging and on-track toward the desired outcome.

All of the above will help define the **5 P's of Preparation**™:

+ **Purpose:** Why are we holding the session? What are the key objectives?
+ **Product:** What do we want to have produced once we are done? How will we know we have been successful?
+ **Participants:** Who needs to be involved, and what are their perspectives?
+ **Probable Issues:** What are the concerns that will likely arise? What are the "gotchas" that could prevent us from creating the product and

achieving the purpose?

+ **Process:** What steps should be taken during the meeting to achieve the purpose, given the desired product, the participants and the probable issues to be faced?

Customize to Maximize™

A meeting agenda is created to guide you and your participants through a designed sequence of steps to arrive at a desired outcome. For any meeting, the agenda must be clear, accomplishable by the group and completed within the allotted meeting time. While a standard agenda is designed with a focus on Purpose and Product, a customized agenda will deal more effectively with Participants and Probable Issues. The agenda should be designed with a "wide to narrow" experience for the participants, that is, early parts of the process should open the participants to a wide range of possibilities as to what could be done, which promotes brainstorming and visioning. Later, steps of the process should narrow the possibilities of what *could* or *should* be done, down to the strategies or recommendations that *must* or *will* be done.

+ **Could** implies no limitations or restrictions. Use "could" to generate the maximum number of ideas.

+ **Should** implies a moral obligation for action, without responsibility for the action. Use "should" when the group is not yet committed to action.

+ **Must** implies that the group should identify only essential items. The number of items will be smaller, and a level of commitment is implied.

+ **Will** implies that the group should only include actions that they are willing to commit to doing. A smaller number of committed actions will result.

Star(t) Power™

Inform the participants about the overall purpose of the meeting by discussing the session objectives and deliverables.

* **Engage** them in the process by giving them a clear vision of the overall result to be achieved and the benefits to them.
* **Elevate** them by discussing the important role they play in the process. (unique contributions, authority that has been given to them, etc.)
* **Integrate** them as early as possible by identifying their personal objectives, the issues that must be covered, the challenges that must be overcome, or some other topic that contributes to the overall goal of the session.

Ask for It

A skilled communicator demonstrates the ability to ask the right questions. These questioning techniques are applied when preparing, starting, focusing, gathering information, building consensus, and in every other stage of steering toward the desired meeting outcome. If you know how to ask better questions, you can help groups come up with better answers.

The Starting Question: What you should ask to begin a discussion - to be used at the beginning of every agenda item to stimulate responses. These questions should use the group's 'language', be more personal - directed at their specific experience, be action-oriented and open-ended. Start with an image building phrase, "Think about…", "Imagine…", "If…", "Consider…". Don't give answers, but set up an image that helps the participants to clearly visualize.

The Reacting Questions: These questions are used to acknowledge, clarify, challenge, confirm, probe and redirect. In short, they are used to react to a participant's response. These questions guide the discussion by asking, not telling. They are:

+ **Direct Probe** to a challenge.

   "Why is that important?"

+ **Playback Question** to clarify what you believe you know.

   "It sounds like what you're saying is…"

+ **Indirect Probe** to provide a way for the participant to clarify.

   "Is that important because…?"

+ **Leading Question** to seek other solutions.

   "Are there solutions in the area of…?"

+ **Redirecting Question** to get the conversation back on track.

   "That's a fair point - are there any others before we move on?"

+ **Prompt Question** to help keep the group moving.

   "We have covered a, b and c - what else might we do to improve…?".

Infect the Room

Energy is the key element towards keeping a meeting engaging, on track and credible. It is imperative to project energy and animation from the very start, which will establish the energy level for the entire meeting. Executive presence is a major component of your ability to command the room. You should be so compelling that no one else speaks when you are speaking and all eyes and ears are focused on you. There are specific times during the day which are particularly low energy - mid-morning, just after lunch and mid-afternoon. During these periods, you should direct questions toward a specific individual as opposed to the entire group and devise a 'recharge activity' (small-group activities or activities requiring movement) to raise the energy level. Praise and applause are additional tools which can help to energize a room. Following breaks it may be necessary to reset the energy level. Remember, enthusiasm is infectious…if you don't have it, the group can't catch it!

Stay Focused

By keeping participants focused, you will be able to significantly increase the productivity of the group, helping them to achieve the desired outcome. At the beginning of each new agenda item, internal summaries (checkpoints) re-excite participants about the benefits of the meeting. Internal summaries can be delivered as follows:

- **Review:** A top-line overview of a specific portion of the meeting.
- **Preview:** A top-line description of what the group is about to do.
- **Big View:** A top-line explanation of how a specific portion fits into the overall mission.

These internal summaries should be extended when re-starting a session on a new day, or after a prolonged break. When giving complex directions, it's important to step through the PDQ's:

- State the **Purpose**
- Give General **Directions**
- Ask for **Questions**

To keep everyone on track as the meeting progresses, label charts, ask extended prompt questions, and ask redirection questions. Use breakout groups with review and reporting techniques to elevate the focus on specific issues.

Marker Management™

It is your responsibility to ensure that key information is appropriately tran-scribed during a meeting in order to significantly raise the level of retention and sustain key points. Major items which could be documented are:

+ **Branding** (framing)
+ **Major Take-aways** (Aha's!)
+ **Decisions** (made)
+ **Actions** (assigned)
+ **Outstanding Issues** (as a result)
+ **Relevant Analysis** (during session)

It is important to write first - discuss second. Write legibly and record only as many words as necessary to ensure comments are clear and stand-alone, and use the 'headline' technique to shorten long comments. To avoid lulls while writing, you should repeat what the participants said as you write, or ask participants to repeat their comment and ask a direct probe. An overly-eager or disruptive participant is a good candidate for scribe.

It's important that when you scribe, you write the participants' actual words, not what you want them to say. You can demoralize the group when you pick and choose what to record (i.e. waiting until several people have affirmed the point before recording it). Don't be a selective scribe. Let them **own** their words and thoughts.

Knowledge Is Power

Skilled communicators use a variety of functions to engage participants in producing high-level information gathering, brainstorming and prioritizing. When gathering information, reactive questions - as opposed to statements - should be used to acknowledge, clarify, challenge, confirm, probe and redirect. When brainstorming, it's imperative not to allow any judgment or analysis to enter the process - keep it brief and energized. When prioritizing, you, as the leader, should define the criteria, control the lobbying period and test for consensus. You must understand the different information gathering and processing functions and have methods for addressing them:

+ **Gathering Facts** (listing)
+ **Categorizing** (grouping)
+ **Inquiring** (questions)
+ **Generating Ideas** (brainstorming)
+ **Prioritizing** (define criteria, test for consensus)
+ **Reporting** (formalizing feedback)

An Ounce (No, A Pound!) of Prevention™

As opposed to 100% agreement - which is often too time-consuming or even impossible, true consensus allows a group to live with decisions and eventually support them. Disagreements occur when there is lack of shared information, different values/experiences or outside factors.

If there is lack of shared information, you need to start with a common reference everyone can agree on, confirm the source of the disagreement, identify alternatives, ask delineating questions (to define and share information), summarize the information and take a consensus check. If the disagreement stems from differing values or experiences, identify the strengths and weakness of alternatives. If necessary, create new alternatives which include identified strengths (merging), and take a consensus check. If outside factors cause the disagreement, it may be necessary to take the issue to a higher source for resolution (i.e., "I'll speak to Human Resources about the possibility," or "I'll have to check with (immediate supervisor) for approval," etc.)

Revolution Equals Resolution™

Dysfunctional behavior is an activity by participants which substitutes their displeasure with the session content, purpose or process, with alternate, and often disruptive, behavior. **It is a symptom, not a cause.** Dysfunctional behavior doesn't 'go away' - it requires specific strategies to diffuse. Prior to any meeting, it's helpful if you can identify such things as:

+ a participant who objects to the meeting
+ anyone who feels he/she stands to lose something as a result of the meeting
+ participants who are not on favorable terms
+ participants who tend to point out problems rather than offer solutions

Strategies to minimize dysfunctional behavior include:

+ setting of ground rules, interaction with particular participants
+ paying close attention to reactions
+ informal meetings during breaks

It's important to be aware of participants who are not speaking, complain or object publicly, complain or object privately, use non-verbal cues indicating lack of buy-in or seem uneasy with the meeting. They may have valid concerns but not know how to voice them - so they behave inappropriately. Routinely resolve behaviors by approaching the participant privately or generally, empathize with the symptom, address the root cause and get agreement.

Unexpected moments (i.e. outbursts) can be handled by requesting the group's permission to detour from the agenda and then encourage discussions which directly address the issue. When people stop engaging in dysfunctional behavior and begin to exhibit functional signs, you should supply reinforcement. You also need to be sensitive to the needs of the group and allow changes and adjustments.

Handle With Care

Special situations such as very small groups, very large groups, conferences, and conference calls require special skills. With small groups, you need to keep your energy at an appropriate level to avoid overpowering the group. Break-out should be avoided and the group leader should 'check in' with participants to see that they are comfortable with the process and flow. For larger groups, the energy level needs to be notched up.

The 5 P's of Preparation - Purpose, Product, Participants, Probable Issues and Process™ need to be clearly identified and break-out leaders must be carefully briefed to ensure quality and feedback. Directions should be simple and employ a greater number of verbal visuals.

For conferences, after developing the purpose and desired outcomes, you need to:
+ define key conditions required to reach these outcomes.
+ define success strategies to address key conditions.

+ engage appropriate speakers.
+ provide opportunities for participants to engage with speakers.
+ seek out and partner with appropriate venues.
+ apply consensus techniques, if necessary.

When planning a conference call:
+ distribute meeting agendas and handouts prior to the meeting.
+ limit the agenda - if it needs to go over two hours, break it up into more than one call.
+ perform preliminary brainstorming - with results summarized and submitted prior to the call.
+ have as many people as possible in a remote location be in one room and on speaker, as this promotes teamwork.
+ create a list prior to the meeting with the names of all participants and their locations.
+ conduct a roll call to identify all participants.
+ explain the purpose of the meeting at the outset of the call. This will get participants energized, inform them of their decision-making authority and involve them with questions that engage.
+ establish a verbal method for consensus checks and publish a recap immediately following the meeting.

Close It

End each session with a four-step closing process:
+ **Review** - the activities performed, participants' objectives, issues, decisions and actions.
+ **Evaluate** - the value of the session and results achieved.

+ **End** - with a call to action and assignment of next steps.
+ **Debrief** - with management or sponsor, identify strengths and areas for improvement.

It's important to thank the participants for their involvement. When your group feels appreciated, there is a greater chance that the participants will buy-in to the decisions made during the meeting. You must remind them of the next steps, including how documentation will be handled and the date, place and time of the next session (if applicable). Send off the participants reaffirming the benefits of the meeting.

CHAPTER 10

Enlist to Lead
Test Yourself!

1. What are three benefits that result from positive group dynamics?

    _____

2. Name three steps a skilled communicator takes to prepare for a meeting.

    _____

3. Why is the "wide to narrow" format for agenda setting a useful tool?

    _____

4. Why and when is it important to use "starting questions" and "reacting questions"?

    _____

5. How does your animation level affect the group?

    _____

6. Define "internal summary". Why is it useful?

    _____

7. Why is an over-eager or disruptive participant a good candidate for "scribe?"

    _____

8. Why is it important to categorize fact gathering?

_____

9. Why should you avoid making a goal of 100% consensus a priority?

_____

10. What is meant by the observation that dysfunctional behavior is a symptom, not a cause.

_____

11. During a teleconference, how can you compensate for the lack of face-to-face contact?

_____

12. Why is it important to thank group members for their participation during a meeting?

_____

11

Great Communicators

"That's as well said as if I had said it myself."
Jonathan Swift

MISSION STATEMENT
Effective communicators mimic
the successful methods of others.

What makes a great communicator? Why was Ronald Reagan considered a master at getting his views across to people? Why is ABC's Diane Sawyer so good at transmitting warmth while always being professional? Why is Rev. Jesse Jackson so compelling? Why do so many viewers trust Charlie Rose?

In this chapter I offer my own totally biased views on great speakers and what we can learn from their strengths. While any roster of great all-time communicators would be headed by such historical leaders as Abraham Lincoln, John F. Kennedy, Winston Churchill, Golda Meir, Martin Luther King, Jr,. Margaret Thatcher and Malcolm X, for the purposes of this book, I'm focusing on more recent examples.

Pope John Paul II

The outpouring of sorrow over the death of a religious leader who was very sick, tired and elderly was a testament to the communication skills of this once humble Polish priest to reach out and emotionally bond with his 'flock'. George Weigel of the New York Post put it best: "When Pope John Paul II died, the extraordinary global outpouring of affection and regard for this old and, in recent years, increasingly crippled Polish priest and bishop suggested that Karol Wojtyla had, in fact, influenced more lives in more diverse circumstances than any human being of his time." Or as Bono of U-2 fame put it, "Pope John Paul II was the best 'frontman' the Church ever had."

Bottom Line: Pope John Paul II made lasting, emotional connections.

Johnnie Cochran

The outpouring of praise for and grief over the pre-mature death of one of the greatest American trial lawyers in recent memory was a testament, not only to his legal skills, but his uncanny ability to successfully serve his myriad of clients with his superb presentation skills. This lawyer turned TV talk show host is arguably best known for his rhyme, "If it doesn't fit, you must acquit." He also had the fastest vocal delivery I've ever heard. Go back and play the O.J. Simpson trial videotapes when Cochran was Simpson's lead defense attorney. His speech pattern is why he was so engaging. Audiences love an energized rate. Not only was Cochran warp speed, he also included calculated, welcome pauses. Cochran held our attention with his rapid-fire delivery, key stressed words and crisp enunciation.

Bottom Line: Cochran had energy that engaged.

Ronald Reagan

The former actor and 40th President of the United States had the best smile, of not just any male, but any public figure. Reagan always put us at ease by speaking in a Midwestern self-effacing style. Being a Midwesterner myself, I can speak with some authority on this. We think the way to be graciously aggressive is to preface everything with filled pauses such as "err," "um" and "ah" so we don't sound too assertive and people won't be intimidated by our thoughts. Reagan's take on that was to preface everything with "well," which made him sound rather folksy.

President Reagan was able to tell a story better than anyone, right up there with Mark Twain and Will Rogers. He had a wonderful way of deflecting and deflating an antagonistic press. Whenever he was asked a negative question during his presidency, he had this uncanny ability to switch gears and say something like, "That reminds me of a story." By the time he was finished with his narrative, the press didn't care that he hadn't answered the question - they were entertained and satisfied.

Bottom Line: Reagan was folksy and likeable.

Katie Couric

Here is an example of a high profile individual we've seen evolve before our very eyes. After a relatively inauspicious beginning as a field reporter on CNN, Katie Couric came to the attention of network executives during her stint at the NBC Washington affiliate. She was brought into The Today Show at age 34 to cover for Deborah Norville during her maternity leave. Katie was an instant hit and the rest is history. She rose to be one of the highest paid journalists in television and contributed greatly to the record-breaking success of The Today Show - NBC's most lucrative program. At age 49, she made the transition from morning show anchor to network news anchor at CBS, signing a reported $45 million, 3-year contract. This did not happen by accident. Aside from her highly polished journalistic skills, Ms. Couric's ability to brand herself as a serious, yet extremely likeable persona caused millions to tune in every morning. As she matured and her credibility evolved, so did her style. Her youthful matronly look morphed over the years into a chic, highly flattering and much talked-about example of superior personal packaging. Coupled with her animated, yet sincere delivery, she became an example and inspiration to young women considering a career in television news. Without being maudlin or self-pitying, she weathered the very public death of her husband and became a champion for colon cancer research. There is no one in television today who better connects with an audience than Katie Couric.

Bottom Line: Couric has infectious energy.

Al Gore...yes, really!

An Inconvenient Truth - while Al Gore will always remain a polarizing figure to some, the truth is he emerged from the wilderness and into the media spotlight a changed man. By returning to a deeper mission - to his life's passion - he found his voice. It is fascinating to observe a public figure of such notoriety go through a profound transformation. Gone is the stiff and preachy Al Gore of the 2000 election cycle. The new Al Gore talks to us (he doesn't lecture!) with true passion about a subject of great importance... and he does it with the aid of a superbly crafted slideshow presentation. His communication style is authentic and engaging.

No matter where one resides on the political spectrum, anyone who cares about becoming a more effective speaker should observe Al Gore "in action" in Davis Guggenheim's film, "An Inconvenient Truth".

Bottom Line: While clearly a master of visual aids, (the new) Al Gore is highly effective because he speaks with confidence and clarity.

Maya Angelou

Maya Angelou is hailed as one of the great voices of contemporary literature and is also a major voice for African-Americans around the world. As an author and speaker she possesses a gift of crafting magnificent prose, and orating with a well-trained instrument, smoothly and with dramatic resonance. You cannot think of this remarkable woman without hearing her unique and definitive intonation, filled with sweeping verbal visuals and dramatic intensity, encouraging all who hear her or read her words, to aspire to live on a higher plane. In a few short minutes, she managed to communicate the idealism, joy and sense of purpose of Bill Clinton's presidency as the poet-laureate of his first inauguration. She is also an award winning educator, historian, actress, playwright, civil-rights activist, producer and director. A hypnotic vision of grace, swaying and stirring when she moves, Maya is an example of someone who has mastered the art of coordinating facial animation, vocal variation and effective movement. Whether speaking to one or many, Dr. Angelou is without peer when it comes to impacting, connecting and communicating.

Bottom Line: Maya Angelou has a voice and is a voice.

Larry P.

Here's someone who isn't a household name, but he should be. Larry is the best corporate speaker I have ever heard. This pharmaceutical executive is terrific at engaging us and taking us through his key points and supporting information. Even when he gets serious, he paints wonderful word pictures.

Probably the most brilliant speech I ever saw anybody give was one Larry delivered to a group of sales representatives. He was then president of a small pharmaceutical company that has now grown into a $3 billion giant. At the time, there was a tremendous morale problem. They were losing sales representatives to their competition, and Larry had to deliver a speech that would keep his sales force together.

He got up onstage and began by asking everyone who wasn't a salesperson to leave the room, "because I want to have a candid discussion with you without any managers present." This was a real "aha!" It spoke directly to the reps and made them feel like he really wanted to connect.

The members of the field force felt a tremendous sense of relief because they knew they could now be candid without their managers on hand to observe them. "I've been where you are," Larry said, "the whole Indian walk in the moccasin thing." "If you don't think I've been there, I'm going to tell you a story to prove my point. It's Sunday night at 7 p.m., you've finished dinner, you're in the family room leaning back in the recliner, your wife is trying to put the kids to sleep, and life is good. Then there's a jolt of reality when the phone rings. It's your manager and he says, 'You know what, I think I'll ride with you tomorrow while you make your calls.' You say yes grudgingly. You try to find a car wash open on Sunday night. You start cleaning your car, you polish your shoes and you get out your tie to look presentable in the morning. This is not the way you want to start the week."

Larry immediately had the audience in the palm of his hand, as he was describing their world perfectly. The man had **rapport with a purpose**™. He was connecting with them at a very base level, with a reason in mind. He used inclusive pronouns. He paced the stage, but not like a caged animal.

He made the reps feel like they were having a conversation with him. And it worked. He kept the company together, just by speaking honestly to them and making them feel that he cared. He convinced them that the company would turn a corner and that the reps would have a voice.

I saw Larry work the same kind of magic on another night, in an impossible-to-win situation. He was then with another company in an even more senior position. Larry was the "big boss" to whom the president of the company reported. The snag this night was that the president couldn't make it to the big national meeting. There were issues with their product that sent him to Washington D.C., to appear before the Food and Drug Administration. The president had to discuss sensitive concerns around safety and efficacy, leaving Larry holding the bag.

Hundreds of people had come to the meeting in Scottsdale, Arizona, and yet there was no president to address them, no one to deliver the bad news. All the other high level executives had left town upon learning the negative turn of events. The only one with the stamina to stay was Larry. The president's subordinate told him that the company would lose everything if he didn't say something great to keep the sales force motivated. "I don't do dinner," said Larry. "You're doing dinner," said the subordinate. "I don't do dinner," Larry repeated.

Finally, the young man prevailed upon him, and Larry P. walked out onstage. He shook his head and said one more time, "I don't do dinner." That immediately caught everyone's attention. "But tonight," he said, "I'm doing dinner. I don't want to be here telling you what I'm about to tell you. I'm mad as hell that I have to make this announcement at dinner. But as it turns out, we can't launch our product at this meeting. The FDA has postponed approval. I believe they are wrong and this company is right. We have good science behind us, and we're going to make sure our protests are heard."

By the end of the evening, Larry hadn't resolved anything, but he had won over the hearts of the room with his passion. The sales force gave him a standing ovation. Larry did what he always does - he connected. He's animated, he paints words with a fabulous road map, he thinks on his feet and is a great raconteur. I have never seen nor heard anyone create better imagery than Larry P. He just has the ability to bond with any audience at any level.

Bottom Line: Larry P. knows how to play to each and every audience.

CHAPTER 11

Great Communicators
Test Yourself!

1. What technique did Ronald Reagan use to deflect negative questions by the press?

   _____

2. Maya Angelou artfully coordinates the use of three distinct techniques when speaking. What are they?

   _____

4. What is the lesson of Al Gore's transformation as a public speaker?

   _____

3. What is it about Katie Couric that compels millions of viewers to watch her and networks to fight over her?

   _____

4. Describe how Larry P. uses "rapport with a purpose" to connect.

   _____

5. Think of someone who you personally consider a "Great Communicator". Identify three things that make them a successful public speaker.

   _____

CHAPTER 11

12

The Golden Rules of Networking

"It isn't just what you know, and it isn't just who you know. It's actually who you know, who knows you, and what you do for a living." - Anonymous

MISSION STATEMENT
*The cultivation of mutually beneficial, give-and take,
win-win relationships will result in a large diverse group of
people who will buy and promote your "brand".*

No book on personal branding would be complete without a chapter on networking, the vehicle by which you can successfully market *you*. Let's face it - success in this world is based on your ability to pursue and cultivate solid relationships. This applies to business as well as personal pursuits. No one is going to hire you, date you or even consider you if you keep yourself a secret. You never know how the person standing next to you can help you in your quests if you don't reach out. You must seize opportunities everywhere, **all** the time, whenever they come your way.

A case in point: I was recently on line at TKTS, the half-price theatre ticket booth in NYC's Times Square - have you seen the prices of Broadway shows these days? Yikes! My daughter is a musical theatre fanatic, so we spend a lot of time at the TKTS booth. This particular afternoon, the line was unusually long, so to pass the time we checked out the people in our vicinity.

As it happened, there was a mother and daughter pair just behind us, so we struck up a conversation. They, like us, lived in the suburbs. The other girl had a passion for theatre too and the other woman had taken a day off from work (as had I) to treat her daughter to a matinee. We carried on a brief conversation on the trials and tribulations of being working mothers and soon, we were at the front of the line.

As we went to different ticket windows, I had no idea which show they were going to end up seeing, but waved to them as we each went off to our respective luncheon destinations. As fate would have it, we ended up choosing the same show and even sitting next to each other! We were pleasantly surprised that our reactions to the performance were so similar (thumbs down from all of us).

During intermission we chatted casually, discussing our respective professions. Whereupon she informed me that her husband was the managing partner of a major law firm in Manhattan. She felt I might be able to do some business with him, impressed that this was the first time anyone on line had bothered to make conversation with her and she felt that her husband's firm could benefit from my professional skills. She would speak to her spouse and have him call me to set up a meeting. From a simple outreach on the ticket line, I ended up booking an important new client!

Networking - it costs nothing and can yield so much. Studies have show that only 10% of jobs are filled through classified ads in newspapers or online recruitment portals. The rest are garnered through personal referrals and placements. Which are you going to trust more when seeking advice on purchasing a product - a commercial or print ad - or a **friend** whose advice you respect?

While some networking can be serendipitous (like my TKTS experience), more often your outreach is carefully strategized with a clear mission in mind. By joining various associations, clubs and societies, you can create contacts with people who can recommend you, hire you, or take advantage of whatever service you have to offer. It might sound trite, but I am a living example of successful networking. All of my clients come to me either from other clients or from those who have personally heard me speak or viewed my CD. I put myself 'out there' at every opportunity speaking to groups, re-visiting existing clients and conversing with those around me during business and personal travel. I also really believe that what goes around comes around and I spend a fair amount of my time recommending talented people to other talented people. I feel good being helpful and in the end, I've built up some insurance for future business by adding to my "implied debt" surplus! Connecting and networking - it's not for the faint of heart but it's essential and an integral part of my business development plan.

To that end, I've created the "Ten Golden Rules of Networking". These will show you the way to appropriately market yourself at any and every opportunity, giving you the ability to get what you ask for, when you need it.

Be Yourself

It is imperative that you develop yourself as a unique brand. Personal branding is the first step toward successful networking. What makes you unique? Why would anyone want to buy from you, listen to what you have to say, take your advice, hire you or secure your services? Like so many iconic brands (Kleenex, Xerox, Jell-O, Tylenol, Scotch Tape), you too can leverage your own brand to set you apart, be noticed, and above all, be desired. Generic products sell, but marketing experts tell us that over 80% of the public prefers known brands because of the confidence they engender and the comfort level they provide. Being a "me too" is a wasted effort! And all that energy is better spent on marketing your brand. Capitalize on the fact that there's no one else like you - your unique qualities will make you memorable. There's an old saying, "If you speak the truth, you don't have to remember what you said." Well, if you're just being you, instead of a "me too", you don't have to think too hard, and you will be remembered.

Apology Not Accepted™

The most damaging four words you can utter while networking are: "Please bear with me." Nobody wants to bear with anybody. And from that conversation, it's the only thing an individual or an audience will remember. You don't want your personal issues to dominate the conversation: ("This cold just won't go away!", "I can't believe I lost my keys again!", "My kids are making me crazy!"). The only way we'll know something is wrong is if you tell us. So don't! Be positive and upbeat.

Don't Be A Victim

Cinderella was helpless without her fairy godmother. Don't wait for yours.™
The often-used expression, "...god helps those who help themselves..." is very wise advice. If you are in a difficult professional situation, you have three choices: you can tough it out and get "used to it", you can effect change to make it better, or you can seek a new opportunity and leave. If your boss berates you or blames his mistakes on you, and you let it continue, he's not going to stop. Do something about it or move on to "greener pastures." (Effective networking can provide you with a potential exit strategy.) If a promised promo-

tion doesn't pan out, speak to the appropriate person or read the "writing on the wall" and look elsewhere. Especially if you've "set the table before you need to eat" with strategic outreach. If others are taking credit for your ideas which you put forth, but failed to sell, your communication/facilitation skills need brushing up. It's easy to be a victim - but you only have yourself to blame.

Say What You Mean

In a world dominated by "political correctness", we often feel compelled to sugar-coat or back-pedal our thoughts and ideas because we fear rejection, or that we'll "offend" somebody. If you don't put yourself out there, you won't be rejected, but you won't be accepted either. Successful networking depends on one's ability to take appropriate and clear stands which will allow you to stand out and demonstrate value. Don't allow your thoughts to be watered down. That will make you instantly forgettable. We like people who have opinions and if you want to stand out in the crowd, express yourself politely but honestly. Saying the popular thing won't make you popular. Management can smell insincerity a mile away. If you pander, you won't be promoted and you certainly won't be rewarded for it. Taking strong stands with the necessary backup information will market you as smart, capable and able to make choices - all hallmarks of executive behavior.

Assertive, Not Aggressive

Asserting yourself doesn't necessarily mean dominating. Being passionate doesn't necessarily translate into being emotional. Use animation to express yourself. Be an advocate for your ideas and thoughts while seeking the input of others. Bombastic speakers who bully during conversations push people away. Animated speakers who express themselves articulately and passionately are remembered and embraced. Avoid the dreaded "upspeak" (ending every sentence as if you're asking a question). While many use this as a way of engaging people and permitting them to disagree, it comes off as empty-headed and annoying. Use effective vocal variation to color your key-stressed words. This draws people to us. Don't be overly pushy or drone either - you'll just push people away. To network successfully, you must engage and persuade, not intimidate or bore.

Vent With A Purpose™

It's very easy to criticize, and a great deal harder to provide effective solutions. A critic adds no value, while a problem-solver is worth their weight in gold. When self-marketing, put yourself in the "role of receivership." Am I giving value to those with whom I am speaking or am I just spouting negativity? Am I providing solutions or exacerbating an already difficult situation by being destructive? If something needs fixing, by all means say so, but also have a fix in mind. Nobody likes being around negative people. Venting for the sake of expressing disapproval accomplishes nothing except possibly making you feel better, which has absolutely no value when networking. Venting along with constructive change makes you a valuable commodity.

Don't Be Invisible

The major impetus behind networking is to be noticed and valued. While you may be valuable, if no one notices, nobody's going to know how valuable you are. Personal packaging is hugely important; dress like a "player." Be animated and engaging. Studies have shown that how you look and how you sound amounts to 93% of the total impact in any communications experience. Think of the last time you were at a meeting or party. Who do you remember and why? Chances are it was someone who packaged themselves with great attention to detail and spoke with animation. In networking, you need to "raise your personal status" as opposed to being totally generic. A keenly developed executive presence will propel you forward and upward. An invisible presence will keep you where you are, or left behind.

Use Inclusive Language

No person is an island and when we network, it's important to speak inclusively. The ongoing use of "I," "Me," and "My," denotes a personal agenda which may or may not have anything to do with anyone else. By substituting inclusive pronouns such as "We," "Us," and "Our", we imply a partnership which engages all those to whom we are speaking. "Well, I think that we should…" is very different from, "Well, we should think about…". "I need to discuss…" is much more isolating than "Let's discuss…". Partnering is a major component of leadership. It speaks of common goals, values and aspirations. It recruits the group to "jump on your bandwagon". You will achieve much more buy-in with "We" than "I."

You Never Get More Than You Ask For

Asking for what we want does not communicate need - it communicates self-worth. We are fearful to ask for too much because we're afraid we'll be turned down. The fact is if you don't ask for what you need, no one is going to give it to you. And, if you don't ask for much, the impression is that you're not worth very much. Don't be unrealistic, but never be afraid to request every bit of what you require, and then some. You may raise expectations and have to produce at a higher level, but that too, will be to your benefit. The more productive you are, the more valuable you become, and you'll be in a better position to ask for even more, give even more and extend your network. Minimize your needs and you minimize your value.

Own It!

Being productive is important, but if you "hide your light under a bushel basket" and nobody knows about it your productivity will not be attached to you which will negatively impact your ability to market yourself. Do the reverse … declare it! If your idea was turned into a lively new concept - let them know it was you who thought of it. Your new strategy streamlined the operation - make sure management hears about it. Your referral proved to be the best addition to the department in years - take it to the top! Modesty may be a virtue in certain circles, but when networking, it's a deadly sin. You don't have to play fortissimo all the time - no one likes a braggart and ownership has nothing to do with volume. It has to do with ensuring that the right people have the right knowledge to give credit where credit is due.

Now, that's a song worth singing!

CHAPTER 12

The Golden Rules of Networking
Test Yourself!

1. What is the most important aspect of successful networking?

    _____

2. What are the most damaging four words you can utter while networking? Why?

    _____

3. Explain why you should be assertive rather than aggressive.

    _____

4. When self-marketing, why should you put yourself in the "role of receivership"?

    _____

5. Why is personal packaging important in networking situations? How does it relate to executive presence?

    _____

6. Define Inclusive Language. Why is it important?

    _____

CHAPTER 12

Final Summary

"Be sincere; be brief; be seated."
Franklin D. Roosevelt

MISSION STATEMENT
Effective communication skills are inter-dependent. They must be used in concert in order for the speaker to impress, connect and engage

Branding oneself is serious business - you need to **create positive halo**™ before you even walk into a room. When you leave, you'll want to be remembered having achieved your desired outcome.

So now that we've spent some significant time together, let me repeat some key takeaways:

+ **Smile**
+ **Package yourself appropriately**
+ **Make your audience happier, smarter or richer**
+ **Use an animated voice**
+ **Move with a purpose**
+ **Give face**
+ **Partner with your venue**
+ **Master the art of visual aids**
+ **Remember: less is more**

George Bernard Shaw once said that "a pessimist is a man who thinks everyone is as nasty as himself, and hates them for it." Radio commentator Paul Harvey once said, "I've never seen a monument erected to a pessimist." Whereas Colin Powell is quoted as saying, "Perpetual optimism is a force multiplier." Don't let the pessimist's way of life take over your body. Be energetic. Stand erect. SMILE!

Metropolitan Life once developed a test for potential employees to sort the optimists from the pessimists. The insurance company went on to discover that optimists outsold pessimists by 20% the first year and by 50% the following year!

Think Positive! Act Positive! Be Positive!

Repetition Builds Retention™

The three main points of this book bear repeating:

- **First.** Make your audience happier, smarter or richer: Audiences listen with vested self-interest. Your executive presence is enhanced when you begin with the audience in mind. Put yourself in the role of receiver ship. Give them a reason to care, and they will.
- **Second.** You're on! The spotlight is always on us. So, dress with attention to detail and impact. Be animated, and leverage body language to its best advantage.
- **Third.** Enthusiasm is infectious - if you don't have it, your audience can't catch it. People remember little of what you said - but do recall how you said it. So, smile and make eye contact - people will feel you're connecting with them. Simply put - Enlist to Lead.

L.E.A.D.™

In essence, **L.E.A.D.** with everything you do:

+ **L = Leadership.** Elevate yourself to the status of **leader** - always with a clear mission. Empower others to participate, make people feel good and get them to act on your information.

+ **E = Everybody.** Speak with your audience in mind, not about your needs. It's about the art of inclusion, a dialog not monologue.

+ **A = Arrive** at consensus and persuade people to see things your way.

+ **D = Direct** the process and get people to act on your ideas. Life is one continuous sales call - buy from me, date me, promote me, elect me, fund my program, underwrite my grant... It's that final moment of the "sales call" when you ask for the order. Offer lots of benefits - not features - and be memorable!

Don't Say Too Much
Say It Well
And Say It Often!™

Appendix

TAMARAISMS

Adjust To Achieve™
Be flexible about the process and firm about the outcome.™

Apology Not Accepted™
Don't minimize or qualify.
Don't start the race by standing in a well.™

Compliment Before You Complain™
Make deposits in their ego bank before making withdrawals.™

Conversation, Not Presentation™
Create a dialogue - actual or virtual - and engage your audience's brain.

Customize To Maximize™
Nobody likes to be generic.

Don't Say Too Much
Say it well, and say it often.™

Give Them A Reason To Care
Consider their needs.
Make your audience happier, smarter or richer. ™

Listen And Build Debt™
You'll get as good as you give.

People Forget Most Of What They Hear - Almost Right Away
Details can be deadly.

Pick Your No's™
Choose your battles.

Preparation Equals Relaxation™
Don't expect the moment to inspire you - it won't.

Rapport With A Purpose™
Establish a relationship with an end in mind.

Rehearsed Spontaneity™
PLAN YOUR PRESENTATION.
Just don't sound like you did.

Repetition Builds Retention™
You can't say it often enough.

Tune Your Trumpet And Play With ALL Of Your Notes
Mix your speaking soundtrack with vocal variety.

When You Think "But," Say "And"™
"And" advances,
"But" is the verbal eraser of life.™

Plan Your Outcome
The beginning's important, the end is everything.

Push The Bumper
It ain't over 'til it's over.